Like the magician in one of his stories, Robert Miltner makes things appear and disappear, amusing and unsettling us at once. These are provocative narratives of working people with all the punch of wit and all the lyricisim of poetry, plus you get to figure out how the titles (all Beatles songs) fit these stories that mostly happen as quick as a sneeze. If you're looking for plot twists and engaging ambiguity, here they are. If you're looking for open endings, characters you may live next door to, or may have had a drink with, or an affair with, or may have heard tell of (a lickerish Johnny Appleseed shows up early, John F. Kennedy later), here they are. If you're looking for poignant and wry situations cast as sudden fictions and prose poems, you'll want to read *And Your Bird Can Sing*.

—Richard Hague, author of *Learning How: Stories, Yarns, and Tales*

OTHER WORKS BY ROBERT MILTNER

BOOK

Hotel Utopia. New Rivers Press. Moorhead, MN: Minnesota State University Moorhead, 2011.

CHAPBOOKS

Imperative. White Marsh, VA: All Nations Press, 2013.

Queen Mab and the Moon Boy. Cleveland, OH: Kattywompus Press, 2011.

Fellow Traveler. Columbus, OH: Pudding House, 2007. [Out of print]

Canyons of Sleep. Philadelphia, PA: Plan B Press, 2006.

Rock the Boat. Cover art by Marc Snyder. White Marsh, VA: All Nations Press, 2005

Greatest Hits: 1987-2002. Columbus, OH: Pudding House, 2004.

A Box of Light: Prose Poems. Johnstown, OH: Pudding House, 2002. [Out of print]

On the Off-Ramp. Stow, OH: Implosion Press, 1996. [Out of print]

Against the Simple. Kent, OH: Kent State University Press, 1995.

The Seamless Serial Hour. Johnstown, OH: Pudding House, 1993. [Out of print]

ARTIST'S BOOKS/FINE PRESS/LIMITED EDITIONS

Eurydice Rising. Designed and hand bound by Marie Dern and Jane Downs. Fairfax, CA: Red Berry Editions, 2013. Edition: 20, signed.

Northcoast, Ohio. Photographs by Lisa Vargas, hand-binding by David McCoy. Massillon, OH: Spare Change Press, 2005. Edition: 26, signed and lettered.

Four Crows on a Phone Line. With Neil Carpathios, Frank Kooistra, and David McCoy. Massillon, OH: Spare Change, 2002. Edition: 100, numbered; 26, signed and lettered.

Ghost of a Chance. Lithographs by Wendy Collin Sorin. Cleveland, OH: Zygote Press/Idlewild Press, 2001. Edition: 10, signed & numbered.

CD OF POETRY AND MUSIC

Two Trains Too Many. Poems by Robert Miltner, music by Erin Vaughn. Canton, OH: Blue Caboose Music, 2012.

SCHOLARLY BOOKS

Not Far From Here: The Paris Symposium on Raymond Carver. Vasiliki Fachard and Robert Miltner, eds. Newcastle upon Tyne, UK: Cambridge Scholars, *forthcoming 2014.*

New Paths to Raymond Carver: Essays on His Life, Fiction, and Poetry. Sandra Lee Kleppe and Robert Miltner, eds. Columbia, SC: The University of South Carolina Press, 2008.

AND YOUR BIRD CAN SING

ROBERT MILTNER

HARMONY SERIES

BOTTOM DOG PRESS
HURON, OHIO

ISBN 9781933964966

Bottom Dog Publishing
PO Box 425, Huron, Ohio 44839
http://smithdocs.net
e-mail: Lsmithdog@smithdocs.net

General Editor: Larry Smith
Layout & Cover Design: Susanna Sharp-Schwacke
Cover Art: Marc Snyder
Author's Photo: Mike Rich

ACKNOWLEDGMENTS

Thanks to the monthly workshop: Shannon Young, Brian Young, and Molly Fuller. Thanks also to the Research Council of Kent State University for a Creative Activity Grant that provided time for writing some of these stories.

Acknowledgments continued on page 117.

Contents

Dedication
For Molly

WE CAN WORK IT OUT

"What you're holding in your hand is an orchard," that's what I tell the old boy who's leaning on the door frame and looking at the seeds cupped in his hand. They could be buckshot, small black tears, burned bits of wood found in front of a hearth.

"Apples to eat all through the fall," I say, "Winesaps, Northern Spies, Virginia Beauties, Foxwhelp or Cox's Pippins to press into cider and let harden. Easy as pie," I say, "or my name's not John Chapman."

He looks at my face, looks away, then looks back.

"Just picture yourself," I say, "warming your plough-weary knees in front of a roaring hardwood fire come January, sipping on that applejack."

Eyes closed, he will see it.

They all do.

Then, jaw set, he'll walk, apples in his eyes, to the barn to find his planting tools, his hammer, saws, and adz to build a cider press.

So busied, he'll forget me.

Meanwhile, I'll go around to his back door, with a red Delicious in each of my hands.

One for his wife, one his daughter, the apples of my eyes.

DRIVE MY CAR

The curve rose from the ribbon of the coastal road and I told her to hold on. All six cylinders of the BMW Z3 purred louder as our speed increased.

Her red hair streamed behind her like a silk scarf, her mouth an open circle. She put her hands on the dashboard and began to sing, loud, louder than an approaching cop car, running scales up the musical pyramid toward a high "A."

The trick was to downshift from fifth to third and lean the hurling steel mass of the car into the sharp turn, rear tires screaming as they grabbed traction and pushed the red-lining engine of the car the way a runner lifts onto his toes to burst into speed.

The car had been engineered in Bavaria just for grinning curves of road like this one. I felt simultaneously exhilarated and calm, though it could have been either her or the ecstasy whispering in my ears that seemed to turn into wings as the night air rushed past me, like a conch shell over the hammer, stirrup and anvil so that the sea roared like a gale.

Over the water the moon was a silver coin I was about to flip, a test of luck in which maybe just this once I'd win the toss after all the times I'd been *this close*.

She put her hand on my hand on the gearshift, the way she'd done at the bar where I'd met her as she pushed my fisted dollars back and picked up the tab for the drinks. Together we downshifted into third and I pushed the gas pedal hard.

The centrifugal force pulled our mouths into contorted grins. Guitars wailed on the radio. I saw the green star glint in her eyes and recognized the quick arrival of desire.

We threw our hands up like we were kids going downhill on a roller coaster, screaming until there was no air left in our lungs.

NORWEGIAN WOOD

Here's the part of the evening that makes a story: I'm having dinner in a chain restaurant of a forgettable name with my second wife's brother and his ex-wife who's in town to pick up a few things she left at the house she left him with. The dinner is arranged and awkward, and my second wife and I are there to keep the lid on old injuries that nobody wants to see boil over. So: the ex-wife is edgy, the brother is conciliatory, my second wife who is to become my ex-wife is broody and quiet as a lonely man's telephone, and I've just finished my second glass of a decent house red and am looking for the server to order a third.

Anyways, as they say in Ohio, the brother-in-law's ex-wife starts telling us that she's an avid gardener, you know, annuals, perennials, designer roses, mulch and stone and ponds and blah blah. "But no god damn tomatoes," she says, snapping it out like that at her ex, my ex-brother-in-law, her eyes dark as Black-Eyed Susans, an invasive bastard of a weed she wouldn't allow in her garden but which she spits at her ex. I don't know. Maybe he likes tomatoes since they might have been the only thing he was able to grow except for mission statements and volunteer rolls and grants. So we go back on topic and talk about gardening because it's safe and it's her turf, and she's the out-of-towner and the ex-est of us all.

Then she says, in this I'm-so-cool way people do when they link themselves with somebody famous, sort of celebrity-by-proxy, that she just returned from a rose gardening seminar. In Province-town. With the famous gardener, Stanley Kunitz.

"Kunitz?" I say. "You mean Stanley Kunitz, the poet?"

"No," she says, in a tone as sharp as piece of broken flowerpot, "Stanley Kunitz, the *gardener*."

"Right, the poet," I say.

But she won't return my volley.

"What?" she says, curious and the center of attention, "You mean sweet old Stanley writes poems?" She's starting to blink now. "Are his poems as good as his roses?" she asks.

"Well," I say, putting my arm over the back of the chair, "They're each in rows, you know. His lines in his poems. His roses in his garden. In lines."

But before she can tell me that roses can be grown in circles and squares and hexagons and Medieval love knots, our salads arrive, and she and I and her ex and my ex-to-be all start forking and chewing like ravenous rabbits, as if the last heads of lettuce on the planet had been herded in circles on our plates for us to eat.

While I'm chewing, I'm thinking that if my second wife's brother's ex and I went to see Stanley Kunitz together, I'd want to get a book signed and she'd want a rose.

But we don't. See him together. We don't ever do that.

Because one thing leads to another and then another and my ex-brother-in-law moves to Seattle, and his ex walks out the door of the restaurant and falls off the planet for all I know. And I told you she was my second wife, so she follows her brother's ex and walks out another door at another time.

Anyways, as my second wife used to say, I stayed in Ohio. And now when I open my copy of Stanley Kunitz's *Passing Through* the damndest thing happens. I smell flowers. I close my eyes and I can see roses in rows straight as verse, roses in squares solid as prose poems, and in rich, metaphoric colors like a garden growing on an artist's palette: newly-fallen-snow white, butter-and-eggs yellow, Georgia peach, candy apple red, love-is-like-a-red-red-rose red, passion red, angry red, blood red, long-gone crimson, the pleasure of a fine poem just read red.

TICKET TO RIDE

Molly loves the dog but Edwin doesn't. She found the puppy on a busy road near school trying to bite the tires on moving trucks. Since the dog's future seemed doubtful and brief, Molly opened the door of her Subaru wagon, and the pooch, without invitation or treat, jumped up into the passenger seat, sitting there as if it was *her spot.*

"What's his name?" Edwin asks.

"*Her* name. It's Prints."

"Like in the artist-formerly-known-as?"

"No, not like that!"

"Freddy Prince, then?"

"No—Paw Prints! 'Cause she's such a cute doggy," Molly replies in baby talk, rubbing her face against the dog's muzzle, to which Prints responds by licking Molly's face. Edwin, seeing the slobber, imagines the places the dog's tongue has probably been and winces.

It disturbs him that his wife, a previously rational person, is speaking to a stray dog in the same cooing baby talk she has always criticized others for obnoxiously doing.

"What a sweet name for a sweet doggie," Molly coos, "Don't you just think so, Edwin?"

"Yes," he says, wearing his best smile, "Sweet."

Edwin takes one look at the mutt, its body looking like a furry dachshund but with the head of a larger animal, a shepherd maybe, or a Saint Bernard, grafted on. Though he doesn't say so, he believes the dog has been made from spare animal parts in someone's basement, then, seen as a failure, dropped off along the road where Molly found it.

Edwin knows an omen when he sees one.

He begins plotting against the dog.

15

*　　　*　　　*

Molly is in the basement, putting a load of darks in the washer, when Edwin initiates his first incident. Rising from the kitchen table, he goes into the bathroom, picks up the trash can, and strews its contents across the floor. Prints watches him, wagging her tail.

Next, he goes into the kitchen, sets the trash receptacle on its side, and pulls out the coffee grounds, some cheese sauce, and a couple of egg shells which he grinds against the linoleum with his shoe as Prints lies on the floor, her eyes following his heels.

Lastly, he hurries to Molly's upstairs office in the extra room. He takes a few stacks of sorted homework papers from Molly's students, and lets them flutter over the floor. Prints sniffs a few of the closest, then trots out of the room. *Excellent*, Edwin thinks, as he considers how many papers Molly has arranged into piles on her desk.

Back downstairs, he sits back down at the kitchen table, reads the financial section, and waits. He's not really holding his breath, but he doesn't exhale. Then he hears Molly laughing down in the basement.

"Edwin," she calls, "come down here and see! Prints has been playing with the basement trash. Isn't it hilarious? What a sweet girl you are—let's get you a treat, Printsy-poo!"

The dog sits in the doorway of the bedroom watching Edwin pull shoes from Molly's closet. A Reebok jogging shoe, a penny loafer, two white high heels, a sandal, leather hiking boots: soon he's surrounded by a tiny mountain range of mismatched shoes. Molly has taken her mother to the mall, so Edwin takes his time.

He holds out a cordovan penny loafer to the dog.

"Here you are, girl," he says, trying to sound friendly. "Want a taste?" He lifts the shoe to his mouth and pretends to chew, making the *tnup-tnup* sound a mother makes when trying to entice an infant to eat. Prints trots slowly over, gives the shoe a brief sniff, then returns to the doorway and sits back down.

Edwin crawls over to the door, a sandal held in his mouth by a strap. He snarls playfully. Getting no response, he decides to play rough to see if Prints will respond, so he swings his head rapidly left to right, back and forth, the way a terrier swings a caught rodent. The sandal bangs against his left ear, his right, then the left one again.

"Son of a bitch," he says as he spits the sandal from his mouth. "You stupid damn dog!"

Prints scoots under the bed and won't come out.

"OK, then," Edwin says, as he starts to chew on one of the white high heels.

After Molly's been home half an hour or so, she goes into the second floor bedroom looking for her slippers. From his leather chair in the den, Edwin hears her stop moving, then notices how silent she is. Edwin grins triumphantly behind the sports page. When he hears Molly quietly enter the room, he looks up. Molly holds a sandal by a chewed, wet strap. Her mouth is tight.

"My god," says Edwin, his concerned tone floating like a dark cloud above his statement, "what happened?"

"Somebody did a job on my shoe. And I know who," she says, looking at the puppy. "And I know why."

"What do you think you should do?" he asks, reminding himself to sound convincingly concerned.

"There's only one thing *to* do," Molly says decisively. "Come on, Prints," she says, "we're going for a ride."

After Molly and the dog drive off, Edwin opens his best bottle of Argentine Malbec. Lifting his glass in a toast to his success, he says, "To Prints, who left no trace." He chuckles while he tastes the rich red wine.

He's halfway through the second glass when Molly comes home, accompanied by Prints who carries a bag of chew toys in her mouth. "Poor baby is teething," Molly reports, "aren't you li'l doggie?" The last of the Malbec leaves a bitter taste in his mouth.

Edwin comes home early from the office. He opens a package of bacon and begins to wrap a rasher around the legs of one of the pieces of wicker porch furniture. Edwin considers chewing at one of the legs of the end table himself, but decides he might get splinters in his mouth. Prints, sleepy from watching him, scratches at the door to wait in the breezeway for Molly's return. Edwin lets her out, hoping she'll run away.

Edwin sees Molly's Lladro collection and the Hummels she inherited from her grandmother. They are locked in a glass curio cabinet, and there is no plausible way he can think for the dog to turn the key. Still, one shattered Lladro might do the trick, he thinks. Agitated, Edwin goes into the small bathroom off the den to relieve his bladder. As he closes the door, he remembers what it was that used to anger his father about a constantly-shedding yappy little dog his mother once owned named Wee Willie.

Edwin stands in the corner of the bathroom like he's a sleepwalking child who has mistaken the corner for a urinal. Then he goes in the living room with its off-white berber carpet. The kitchen is next on Edwin's rounds; the water-on-linoleum sound starts him giggling like a naughty child who expects never to get caught.

He's interrupted by the kitchen door swinging open as Molly and Prints bound in, Molly laughing, before they stop and Molly stands silent. Edwin stops urinating, hears the stream taper down to a dribble. In the silence that follows, he watches the line of pee stretching slowly across the linoleum like the liquid shadow of a melted popsicle. Prints barks at him and runs from the kitchen. Molly follows.

During the salmon fillet and asparagus dinner that Edwin prepared, Molly chews her food hard. She sits across from Edwin at the small kitchen table. Prints sits next to Molly at the table, her food bowl in front of her. It appears as if she is smiling, but it is just the way her mouth is shaped.

The dog eats small scraps of the fish that Molly feeds her from her plate. Between bites, Molly pets the dog's head and strokes her neck. Her clucking noises makes Edwin think of hens.

Edwin grinds his teeth as he masticates, accompanied by the sound of wet slaps of Prints' tongue as she licks her snout. The overhead ceiling fan lights grow brighter as the sun sets, turning the open windows into dark rectangles. A wall of silence constructs itself between Edwin and Molly. By now, Edwin's had enough: it is time to be decisive.

"You're just going to have to choose between us," asserts Edwin, setting down his fork and folding his arms across his chest. "It's me or the dog. That's all there is to it."

Molly holds out a small roasted red potato to Prints, whose teeth snap shut on it as if it were a bee. Edwin flinches. Molly's laugh bursts from her mouth like a small firecracker.

"Well then," Molly says, bringing her arm around the dog's neck as she puts on her best smile, "that might be easier than you think."

Prints turns her heard first to Molly, then to Edwin, then back to Molly. Her tail, curling down behind her, looks like a comma.

BLACKBIRD

Dear Ms. Emily Dickinson:

Thank you for your interest in the adjunct position teaching poetry in our MFA program. We had an exceptionally strong pool of applicants for the position this year again. I write to regretfully inform you that your experience and credentials were not a good match for our program at this time; therefore, the search committee will not be contacting you for an interview.

Do know that your lack of teaching experience was not an obstacle. Many of our faculty were, in fact, recent MFA graduates who had not taught prior to joining our program. Most of our other candidates, however, have had at least one book with a major publisher, won several contests, received NEA or state art grants, or attended a number of the prestigious summer workshops which are available for those who like to "get away" in order to write. In your case, less than even a handful of regionally limited magazine publications, while commendable in their own right, were not strong enough for us to further consider your application. Your writing sample—of a hand-sewn packet of poems—while certainly artistic, was hardly suitable for a program of our caliber and national-ranking.

In order to expand your potential for future publications, you might consider enrolling in a class at a local community college or in a non-credit workshop at your local library. At the very least, I recommend a grammar and punctuation review class.

Enclosed is a brochure for our Summer Institute. Our instructors are degreed and well-published authors with excellent media contacts, and a number of successful literary agents will be available to review your manuscripts to discuss movie and action-figure rights. Consider attending so you can develop an effective marketing plan for your poems. Limited partial scholarships are available, provided your application is accompanied by letters of reference from at least three former poetry teachers.

Thank you again for your interest in a teaching position in our program. Good luck with your future poetic pursuits.

Sincerely yours,
MFA Program Director

GET BACK

When the glacial scrapes ended, one chunk of glacier was left orphan here. Heavy, it impressed; melting, it became lake. Rain water collected and cooled in its deep, mosses rugged its surface: it turned bog.

Press your hand or foot here (the cause) and look how that tree starts to quake (the effect) over there. Jump once and it's like a free ride at an amusement park; jump twice and your body could break through in silence and sink. Tough as finding the truth in some spots, elsewhere it's weak and shifty as a lie. A car, if anyone was crazy enough to drive across the bog, would be swallowed whole, its entry a scar that would heal clean.

And years and lives from now, when some get-rich-quick land developer drains the bog, what will he find? A partly rusted car. A driver, a teenager no longer looked for, seated but stiff as a statue. Hands still gripping the wheel. Upon his water-mummied face, a grin like a large mouthed bass.

You remember. You saw him on the cover of the tabloids at the checkouts the other day. He looked like any one of a dozen pictures from your old yearbook. Like that kid you used to sit next to in study hall. The one whose name you knew, but whose face you could never recall.

Strawberry Fields Forever

Teddy McArthur loved Christmas. Even in the heat of July he could close his eyes and picture an evergreen tree with its glowing lights, beautiful and colorful ornaments, and sparkling tinsel, smell the scent of pine and cookies, and sing the words to his favorite songs. Teddy thought that even if you added up Easter, the Fourth of July, and his last birthday when he turned eight, Christmas was still better. This would be his first holiday in the new house.

While Teddy's parents and his older sister Terri loved the new house, he wasn't sure. The suburban brick ranch, with its two car attached garage and back yard patio, finally gave them the room they needed, his mother said. The third bedroom was to be a den that could double as a guest bedroom when family from the old neighborhood in the city came to visit.

When asked if he liked the new house, Teddy always said she did, but he didn't mean it. He missed the front porches, Mrs. Engle next door on one side, Grandma Flossie on the other, and his cousins, Larry and Tommy, who were close to him in age, just three doors down. He could walk there himself. He remembered the huge silver maple trees on the tree lawn and the sounds of delivery trucks and fire engines.

But this new house was in a development, the houses were farther apart, and there weren't many kids his age to play with. Hardly any of the lots in Maplewood Estates had trees. The sound he heard most was sprinklers watering the newly-planted lawns.

School ended early on Wednesday. Since it was the start of Christmas vacation, all the children gathered in the auditorium at eleven o'clock. Teddy joined in singing "Oh Little Town of Bethlehem," "Silent Night," "Away in a Manger," "Oh Come All Ye Faithful," and

"It's Beginning to Look a Lot Like Christmas." Father Doyle passed out cellophane-wrapped candy canes as Sister Mary Joy led the singing. When they were finished, the Sisters had all the children lined up for a drink at the water fountains then went into the lavatories to wash the stickiness of the candy canes from their hands. *With a corn cob pipe and a button nose*, the boys sang, their voices echoing against the glazed bricks in the boy's lavatory, until Sister Moira called in to them to stop. But Teddy sang to himself all the way back to the classroom for dismissal, *Take a look in the five and ten, glistening once again.*

When his row was sent to the coatroom to get ready to go home, Teddy found his winter coat, scarf and mittens, then snapped the clasps on his rubber boots which he'd put on over his shoes. He was eager to get home. His sister Terri would probably be in her room, singing along with her 45s spinning on her record player. Usually she listened to Elvis singing *Don't you step on my blue suede shoes*, or Chubby Checker singing *Come on Baby, let's do the Twist.*

"Even Jackie Kennedy does the Twist," Terri told Teddy.

"That doesn't mean I have to," he said.

The past week she had been walking around the house singing *I saw Mommy kissing Santa Claus underneath the mistletoe last night.* Ugh, he thought. He liked Frosty with his corncob pipe and button nose.

His father had taken the day off from the office to help set up and decorate the Christmas tree, and his mother had said she would have Christmas cookies ready when he got home. Teddy could hardly wait to walk into the house filled with the scent of ground almonds, vanilla, and cinnamon. Every year his mother let him have the beaters after the mixer had blended the dough, and he licked the knife after they spread the colored frosting on the cookies. In the cold, waiting in line for the bus, he could taste the butter and sugar on his lips.

When Teddy burst in the door of the house and entered the kitchen, his mother was sitting at the kitchen table turning the pages of *Vogue*. She looked up, and smiled.

"Merry Christmas vacation," she said with a laugh.

Teddy smiled back, but something was wrong. There were no wax paper lined tins filled with cookies on the countertops. No wondrous odor of cinnamon or spices. No oven warmth to greet his cold nose and ears as he removed his mittens, scarf, boots, and coat.

"Where are the Christmas cookies?" he asked.

"Over on the counter," she said, pointing vaguely behind her as she looked at an ad in *Vogue* for Chanel. "I bought a couple of boxes of them at the supermarket," she said, looking up at Teddy with a smile. "They had lots of your favorites—pressed cookies, frosted and sugared. They even had Russian tea cookies and vanilla bean cookies."

"But I thought you were going to make them at home," Teddy said. "I wanted to frost them and lick the beaters, like always."

"Oh Honey," she said, "It saves so much time to buy them. These look just as good. And I can make cookies any old time," she added, getting up and bringing the boxes of cookies over the table and opening them. "Sit down and I'll get you a nice glass of cold milk."

Teddy sat down and looked at the cookies. He picked one up. It looked like cardboard. It smelled like an eraser. It tasted like chalk.

"See?" his mother said, pulling up a chair next to him. "They taste just like mine. And no dishes or pans to wash. Just a box to throw away. Isn't it wonderful?"

Teddy smiled for his mother. He wanted to make his mother happy, even though he didn't feel that way himself. He felt like he had the time his sister Terri told him he wasn't a real McArthur because he was adopted. Though he laughed along with her, it wasn't a real laugh and he knew it.

He watched his mother who had returned to flipping the pages of *Vogue*. Her index finger on her left hand was tapping to the rhythm of his sister Terri who was in her room singing along with the radio. *What a bright time, it's the right time to rock the night away. Jingle bell time is a swell time.*

And then he remembered the Christmas tree.

*   *   *

Every year when the tree was up in its stand, the colored lights, bright tinny ornaments, and tinsel added, Teddy's father lifted him up and held him while Teddy put the gold star on the top of the tree. Sometimes he was nervous as his father set down his highball and lifted him. Teddy felt his father's arms quiver a bit as he lifted the star higher, over the top of the tree, then placing it on the top as if it were a cap. His mother and sister would clap while his father brought him down and set him on the floor, rumpling the hair on his head. *Oh Christmas tree, Oh Christmas tree,* they would all sing, *How lovely are your branches.*

Then mother would bring hot cocoa and cookies into the room. One by one each of them—Father, Mother, Terri, and Teddy— would leave the room, returning with the presents they had wrapped to place under the tree. Mother would turn off the lamps, bathing the room in the glow of the tree lights reflected off the ornaments and the tinsel. For Teddy, this was the most magical moment of the whole holiday season. Even when his mother pinned Christmas cards to the curtains, Teddy would look at the cards that had decorated trees on them.

"None of them will be as good as our tree, will they Mother?" he asked her the day before.

"Everyone thinks their own tree is prettiest," she said.

"As long as it's a Christmas tree, it doesn't really matter what it looks like," Terri added.

His father grinned and nodded his head in agreement.

As Teddy left the kitchen, he sang *But the prettiest sight to see is the holly that will be on our own front door.* He stopped walking and singing the moment he entered the living room.

There was no Christmas tree there. No pine decorated with lights. No ornaments. No tinsel.

Instead, there was a six foot tall silver cone. It looked like it was made from a stick and tin foil. About a dozen dark blue round ornaments were scattered at various places around the tree. It didn't even have a decorated tree skirt. The tree just wasn't real. He started to laugh, but stopped himself.

"What do you think, Champ?" his father asked. He was sitting on the raised hearth in front of the fireplace with its metal sculptures of flying ducks. He was drinking a highball and smoking a Chesterfield.

"We're the first ones to have one," said his mother who had followed him into the living room.

"Watch this!" his father said, bending down near his feet.

Teddy heard a whirring sound and the tree was suddenly bathed in soft blue light. But just as the blue light colored the tree, yellow light appeared, followed by green and red. Then it began to turn blue again.

His father snorted another laugh. He took a puff of his cigarette and said, "You think that's something?" He reached near the base of the tree and, as more whirring was heard, the whole tree began to rotate. As it turned in circles, the color wheel went from yellow to green to red to blue.

His father was playing a trick on him and Teddy didn't like it. His eyes burned and his throat had a bitter taste. He couldn't look at his father or the awful tree.

"What's the matter, Honey?" his mother asked, putting her hands on his shoulders as she stepped up behind him.

"This isn't our Christmas tree," he replied sullenly.

"No, Honey," his mother said, "This is what's new this year. It's an aluminum tree."

"I hate it," Teddy said, folding his hands across his chest.

"Don't be such a square," his sister said from the doorway.

Teddy turned and started down the hallway to his bedroom.

"Are you going to get your presents to put under the tree, Honey?" his mother asked.

Teddy didn't answer. He heard Elvis singing *You'll be alright, in your Christmas of white* as he passed his sister's room. He kept walking.

*　　　*　　　*

After he closed the door to the den, he carried the chair from his mother's sewing machine to the open closet and used it to reach the box of Christmas ornaments that was up on the shelf. Inside he found the glass ones that grandma Flossie had given them, the three he had made at school from egg shells, and the reindeer made from Popsicle sticks his mother had bought at a church Holiday Fair the year before. They fit inside his school lunch box that he had brought in the den. He quietly left the room and went down the hall toward the kitchen.

"What are you doing with your lunchbox, Teddy?" his mother asked.

"I have my toy soldiers in it," he said. "I'm going to take them out and play in the snow with them."

"Fine, Honey, but don't stay out too long, you'll catch cold," she said, flipping the pages of *Redbook*. "And remember your scarf."

"I will," he said, heading toward the mudroom just off the kitchen.

When he was outside, he went around to the front of the new ranch house. There were no trees in the yard, but there was a small evergreen shrub planted near the corner of the house, just past Teddy's window.

Teddy opened the lunchbox. A few snowflakes were starting to fall. Teddy put about a dozen ornaments on the shrub. He had only about twenty pieces of tinsel and he put those on too. Then he looked at the gold star that used to go on the top of the Christmas tree. Because there was not a top to the shrub, he laid it flat on the top, then reconsidered and leaned it against a branch. No one would see it from the street, but he could see it. By the time he was finished, it was snowing harder.

Through the falling snowflakes, Teddy walked over to the living room window and looked in. He could hear music, *jingle bell swing and jingle bell ring, snowing and blowing up bushels of fun*. His father was leaning over near the fireplace, a highball in his left hand, as his right hand lighted the gas log fireplace. His mother and sister moved to the center of the room where they began to do the Twist, their arms moving from side to side as if they were drying their backs with towels. They were laughing and talking. The aluminum tree was rotating and turning, bathed in yellow to red to green to blue light.

Teddy closed his eyes and whole scene stopped, all motion frozen. It all became a Christmas card. He opened his eyes. He leaned toward the window. He put his nose against the glass.

SAVOY TRUFFLE

Will wakes up from his after-lunch nap with his head aching, throbbing as if his head is a wooden post someone is whacking a baseball bat against. And Jody's head hurts too. The cords in the back of her neck feel taut, almost to snapping. Could it have been that double vodka with cranberry juice she was drinking while she fell asleep to the Home Shopping Network?

The New You Store at the nearby mall is always open, so they drive over in their leased BMW SUV. Will parks next to a Hummer because he likes how it looks like an armored Brinks truck.

"I'd like a new head," Will tells the sales clerk at The New You Store. "Me too," adds Jody, "I want a new head, and some perky new breasts!"

Will looks at heads that come with sunglasses, ones that come with a short goatee, but settles on one with smooth skin and a healthy head of thick brown hair that will fit well inside his E*TRADE ball cap.

Jody says, "I don't care what head I get, as long as it doesn't have saggy jowls. I hate that, when the jowls sag," she adds, "It makes me look like Phil Collins looks in those videos."

Bodies are on sale that day, too: slim thighs, smiles, six-packs of abs, pre-pierced navels. Jody gets a pair of slender hands with long fingers and perfectly manicured nails while Will gets a flat tummy since they'll take his beer-belly in on trade (two for the size of one). And Will just can't pass up picking up a set of runner's calves—they'll look so good standing there between his jogging shoes and shorts. His eyes keep turning to look at the pierced nipples, but he decides to wait.

Will and Jody go back home to the new two story house in their development, Willow Crossing, surrounded by oceans of grass and no trees, looking carefully for their house number so they can tell their house apart from the others on the block.

As they enter, a golden retriever whose name they don't know—*Hello Boy*, they say—waits in the living room, tail thumping the hardwood floor like a metronome that keeps time for the soundtrack of their lives.

In the garage, a new Lawnboy tractor, all gassed-up, waits, ready to roar and purr. The grass gleams a Chemical fertilizer green. The sun shines in the endless blue sky. As their neighbors drive by and see them in the yard that afternoon, Will on the Lawnboy, Jody in the lawn chair, they look good enough to be in a commercial.

Yellow Submarine

Tom Jenks turns the ignition key on his faded blue Plymouth Reliant but nothing happens. He assumes it's just a bad turn of the key, so he tries again, hears a *click-click-click-click-click*, like something failing to connect, hears in the *click-click-click* a mechanical laugh. He's got an appointment in downtown Lakewood for the Weston Building renovation project, and, unless he can get his car up and running in the next ten minutes, he'll be late with his painting bid, *And you know what kind of an impression that makes*, he reminds himself.

Slamming the car door shut, Tom hears the window rattle as a fine red dust sifts from the rust patch on the lower door down onto the driveway. He walks into the attached garage of the light blue bungalow, then through the door leading to the small rose-colored eat-in kitchen where he finds his wife.

Ginny is drinking a glass of Almaden wine from the two liter wine box she keeps on the top shelf of the refrigerator, next to the milk. She's smoking a Camel Light and watching Youtube reruns of *The Young and the Restless*. Now that their own girls are grown and married, she has to have someone else's lives to worry about. Without looking away from the nine inch portable tv set up on the counter between the microwave and the Mr. Coffee Twelve Cup, she asks what he's doing back so soon.

"Car won't start," he tells her. "My *Reliant*," he says, with a grim laugh.

"So why don't you take my car?" she asks.

Tom looks out the window above the sink at the Kowlarski's house, at the new silver Camry parked in their driveway under the shade of the tall oak tree. He thinks about taking Ginny's Vista Cruiser wagon, but it's a land barge, ought to have an Evenrude outboard boat motor bolted onto the back bumper. He doesn't mind piloting it around on these wide suburban lanes, but moving through the tight channels of the city streets, the difficulty of parallel parking a vehicle which takes up the *entire* parking spot leaves him feeling reluctant.

"I'll have you give me a jump start instead," he says.

"How?" she asks, her eyes with puffy upper lids starting to blink, "How do I do that? I don't know how to *do* that."

"It's easy," Tom assures her, making sure to smile to calm her, level her anxiety so she'll pay attention. "I'll push my car out into the street. Then you get your car out of the garage, back it up the street, and get behind me. When you get your car up to about, oh, 35 or 40 miles an hour, I'll pop my clutch—that ought to kick it over, and I'll just go on from there. Got it?"

"Got it," Ginny replies with a set of blinks that remind Tom of Morse code.

Because his car is midsized and the driveway goes slightly down the street, Tom is able to easily push the Reliant down the driveway. The driver's side door is open, and with the car's slow-rolling momentum, Tom is able to scoot around from the front of the car to just behind the open door. Walking slowly backwards, he reaches in, grabs the steering wheel, pulls it sharply to the left so that the car angles, arcing smoothly off the driveway apron and on to the street where it glides slowly to a stop. *Nice*, he tells himself.

As he's getting in, Ginny's dull yellow station wagon backs out of the garage and down the driveway, swings wide around Tom's car, and begins backing up the street, its transmission whining that high reverse *whir*, like an electric mixer on *whip*.

While he waits for his wife to nose her car up to his back bumper, Tom, seatbelt fastened, sits ready: his left foot has the clutch pushed in to the floor, his right foot rests easily on the gas pedal, his right hand grasps the eight ball he's put on the stick shift, his left wrist rests on the steering wheel so that his hand hangs over like a wounded bird. *This is good*, he thinks, *This is good. I'll get my bid in on time.*

He gazes through the front windshield, observes the well-kept lawns of the nestled post-war pastel bungalows much like his own, the grassy shallow ditches which border Oakwood Ridge Road, the huge old trees which bathe the yards in cool shade, even in the dog days of August in Ohio. Tom likes the quiet of his neighborhood, how uneventful life is. *There is something to be said for predictability*, he muses, thinking of how his car's not starting like this is some kind of bad luck. Then he wonders, *What's keeping Ginny?*

Tom looks up into his rearview mirror.

Ginny isn't nosing her car up to his rear bumper. Instead, she has backed up 200 yards and begun accelerating toward him, gaining speed, gripping the wheel, earnestly trying to hold the speedometer needle at around 40 miles an hour for when her car reaches his.

Ginny has misunderstood him: while he thought he described jumping the car much like pushing a child on a sled, she imagined something more like a cue ball breaking a rack of pool balls, like a pop tart—*ping!* —launching out of a toaster.

Tom winces his eyes shut, bracing for the impact. He imagines seeing her face: set, determined, her eyes blinking as rapidly as the flashing lights on an emergency vehicle.

MATCHBOX

His desire is gasoline, her dream a flame. He cracks boxes open, stokes wood, pokes ashes. Sparks ignite the tinder of her lips, crackle the kindling of her kisses. With each whisper, each breath, the embers glow brighter.

Audible to her ear alone is the impulse, the insistence in his voice. This is the kind of air on which she thrives, the kind of fire he feeds.

By moonlight, match light, candlelight, firelight, he loves to watch her dance. With the cool beauty of blue flames, she starts to move. First she is the yellow of ballet, soon the orange of a sultry tango, next the bright red of swing, then the pulsing throb of a colorful nightclub crowd excited by its own force as it bursts out of the doors and starts to dance in the streets.

His breath is a bellows as his cheeks redden, inflaming the glow of his telltale face until, sudden as a siren, he recedes to the anonymity of the shadows. He is wallflower, she is the star under the stage lights. Only his eyes continue to hold her fire.

And when it all comes down to ashes, as it always does, she will again be lye. He'll boil water. Then scrub his hands until the friction makes his skin burn.

While My Guitar Gently Weeps

The year I was fifteen I picked up a paper route to earn some money so I could buy a bright red electric guitar with three shiny pick-ups and start a rock and roll band, *yeah yeah yeah*. I was a sports kid, a jock-o who'd gone over to the troubadours.

Each morning I was up, like an altar boy or choirboy, to serve the daily news, the dollar Dionysus. Papers in the mailbox. Papers in the letter-chute. Papers under doormats, between storm door and inside-door, on rooftops. Paper for Mr. Dow, on the passenger-side seat of his car, who tipped me a dollar a week extra for that.

There were three pretty young girls on the paper route who I knew and I dreamed about collecting from them. Moms at the door, crow's footed-eyes, too much or not enough make-up. Dads at the door, bellies like sails full with wind, cargoed in remembrances they'd tip with.

One day one of the girls (What do names matter now? They are all the same in my memory) came to the door. She had hair to comb and a phone to hold to her ear. She smelled floral and new through the screen. Transistor radio with ear-plug. Her gum bubbled. She pressed the money into my hand, holding it there long enough for it to seem like a money-hickey.

Once, one sort-of-younger woman with an easy-crying baby and a husband absent often in his company car invited me in from the cold for hot cocoa. She talked huskily and fast and chain-smoked cigarettes she lit from the butt of the one just done and cried along with her baby and touched my hair a lot and, as, the afternoon darkened toward the evening, I said I had to go, and so she hugged me really tight a long time against her (my head between her breast, smell of talcum and lake shore) and gave me a twenty dollar tip and a smile as she locked the door behind me. I put the twenty back in her Sunday paper along with a holy card of Mary Magdalene—what did I know then? What do I know now?

Was it was all for cash, for legal tender to exercise my purchasing power for forbidden cigarettes, for magazines I could buy downtown in the bus depot as long as I was tall enough to put the dollars on the counter, and for plastic models of cars built evenings in the basement, goofy from the glue I used?

My year with the paper route I was so cool. I bought that shiny red guitar and the girls loved me. I had a pocketful of coins that talked as I walked. I was like a relatively successful third world country.

BABY, YOU'RE A RICH MAN

Clarence, I used to think the three best sounds in this wonderful life were plane engines, train whistles, and anchor chains. When I was a kid working at the soda fountain, I wanted to take my big old suitcase and have adventures just like Tom Sawyer and Huck Finn. Or be like those guys with the National Geographic Society who went and wrote about giraffes and gorillas and giant sea turtles. Everybody, even Mary, heard about how I was going exploring someday, see those coconuts right there on the palm trees in Fiji and Tahiti. I even planned to work my way across the ocean on a cattle boat to Venezuela where they'd need a man like me with experience in the construction and oil business. I'm not so sure anymore. Not after tonight. Now the sounds of train whistles and plane engines don't pull me away, they bring me back.

When they all came in—Uncle Billy, my brother Harry, Mr. Martini, Burt, Ernie, old man Gower, even Violet—emptying all the cash they could spare into that basket, everything changed. Everyone pitching in to keep the Savings and Loan from being taken over by the big banks, places that pay out to their investors, to people who don't even live here and don't care about our lives, just about how much money bulges their pockets, yelling *I wish I had a million dollars—hot dog!* every time the checks arrive.

Sure, Bedford Falls is just a little one-horse town, and Bailey Savings and Loan is playing nurse-maid to working men and their families—to miserable failures, as Old Man Potter used to call them, but he ought to know, because *he's* one himself—but we are not failures. We are all in this together, just local folks working together to help themselves, serving people who just have to find a way to cover their needs, not giving their profits to some dried-up old man like Potter who wants to keep people in the slums and who has more than he needs anyway. When we work together, nobody has to crawl to the Potters of the world. I was wrong about poor Zuzu's teacher: she should be paid as much—no, more—than that old skin-flint Potter makes in a year. What does he do anyway, just count his money? And where did he learn to do that, beside from a teacher?

After tonight, it makes me realize that people, all people, not just me and Mary and the kids, are more important than profit. That when we help each other, we'll all be rich. Not just here, in this country, but in other places, too—even Venezuela. So I don't know about you, Clarence, but every time a working person gets a chance, I hear a bell ring. And that's the fourth best sound in the world.

Rain

"And another thing about my old man," Angie says out of the clear blue sky that is actually a hazy gray. She's been doing this for the last few months now, since her father died out in Arizona, trying to deal with his dying by talking her way through her unresolved issues. That's her signature segue: And another thing about my old man.

"One card in eight years," she says. "For my sixteenth birthday. Like it meant something to *him*. You know?" she says, adjusting her sunglasses, "and you should have seen the card. I'll never forget it:

This birthday card is just to say,
I hope you have a special day.

Christ—it had a clown with a big dopey painted-on smile. What a pile of crap. Like he remembered for a second he had a daughter and then ran into some awful store and just yanked a card of the rack and mailed it."

Angie and I are in the yard on lawn chairs, lying on our backs. She has rubbed a strong sunscreen on, but I've used one of those tropical tanning oils that smells of papaya and coconut. I smell like a fruit salad. I'm thinking this is what meat must feel like when it is slathered in marinade. We glisten in sweat in the humid July weather of Ohio.

I'm watching the sky while I listen. I can see dark clouds forming and moving in from the northwest. The summer started normal, but for the last two months we've had barely any rain. And though clouds come and clouds go, it seems we couldn't buy a rainstorm even if we had a credit card for the weather.

"And another thing about my old man," Angie says, "is how he signed the card: *Your dad.* Just that. Not *Love, Dad* like real fathers do, but *Your dad.* Like he was trying to distinguish himself from all

45

the other dads in the world, you know? Well", she says, running her right hand through her thick brown hair, "I guess he did."

"Did what?" I ask.

"Distinguish himself from other dads," Angie says.

I think about my father. A gray ghost who was always there but was never there, a cardboard cut-out father who represents to Angie what a real dad is. One Who Is There. Period. I try to picture myself as her dad, a weak drunk who took off. Crying in his beer and missing his kid back in Ohio.

"Maybe," I say carefully, "he bought the card at another time."

"What do you mean?" asks Angie in a wary tone.

"What if he bought it for you on another birthday," I say, watching the clouds thicken, "An earlier one. Maybe when you were nine or something. Because he missed you. But he didn't send it."

"Why would he do that?" she snaps.

"Maybe he was embarrassed. Maybe he felt like too big a shit. Maybe it scared him to care. I don't know. I mean, so what if he saved it in a drawer? And then, when you were sixteen, he sent you that card, the one he'd saved in a drawer. A special card. What if it happened like that?" I ask.

I look over at the silent space occupied by Angie. She has turned on her side toward me, her lips pursed like she does when she knows what she wants to say but knows she shouldn't. She uses her index finger to slide her sunglasses down her nose so I can see her eyes. I do. Blue. Dyed Easter Egg blue. Prom Dress Blue. Early-in-the-morning-on-a-sunny-summer-day blue. Serious blue.

"What if it didn't happen like that?" she says slowly, "What if it didn't?" She turns on her back again and looks up at the gray sky.

We lay there, quiet. I hear a fly or a yellow jacket buzz between us.

"It's *Love*, isn't it?" I say.

I hear her turn on her side again. "What do you mean, *love*?" she asks, her tone bruised, raw. "Do you mean did I love him? Do you mean did he love me? Of course I loved him. He was my father."

"I know that," I say, answering a question I wasn't asked. "That's not it. You're upset that he didn't live up to your expectations, that he only signed that card *Your dad.* You're upset that he didn't sign that card *Love, Dad.*"

Angie doesn't say anything. Behind her sunglasses, I picture her starting to cry, but I know she won't. She doesn't. She holds everything in.

"You're upset that he never told you he loved you," I add carefully.

"No, you're wrong," Angie says, catching her breath. "He did."

"When?" I ask.

"When he called me from the hospital, just before he died," she says. "I told him I loved him. And he told me he loved me. He told me first. Before I told him. *Before* I told him, get it? So I know he did."

"You didn't tell me that," I say. "You didn't tell me that when it happened."

"I couldn't tell you," she says. "I was too embarrassed."

"Embarrassed?" I say. "Why would your telling me you told your father you loved him embarrass you? I think that's a beautiful thing, saying it like that."

"I was embarrassed because it wasn't what I wanted to say," Angie says, practically in a whisper. "I said that because I had to say it. Not that I didn't mean it," she adds earnestly. "But it wasn't what I wanted to say. It wasn't what I wanted to say at all."

"What else was there to say?" I ask. "I mean, he was your father and he was dying."

"I wanted to tell him to go fuck off," she says. "I wanted to tell him to go fuck himself for all the years and hours he kept himself from me. For all the nights he sat around talking with a glass of beer instead of with me. And for all the nights I cried in my room with the TV set turned up so no one could hear me. That's what I wanted to say: *fuck you.* And all I could say was *I love you.*"

Angie is silent. I roll over and can see how the sweat from her hair line and temples runs down the sides of her face, slowly dripping off her cheeks.

And I see rain on her face too. A few drops. Then more. Then a lot. The rain runs from her the top of her head, down behind her glasses, and onto her face. There is a downpour and we are in an outdoor shower, getting soaked.

But we don't move. We lay in our lawn chairs, the rain beading on our oiled bodies and rolling off. We lay still. This feels good, the rain running down our bodies, beading up on our sunglasses.

"We sure needed this rain," Angie says, as I feel her take my hand.

I want to tell her this is what we needed, rain. And honesty too. And that it didn't matter what she said to her father. That they spoke at all is what mattered. And that I think she is being stubborn. Fuck you is what I want to tell her instead.

"Fuck you," I say.

"I love you too," she says.

Hard Day's Night

Janine hates it when things change. Moving makes her act especially stressed: she'll have to double up on Xanax for the week before, and probably for several days afterwards. She's been nesting all her precious things in crumpled newspaper and bubble wrap to avoid breakage with the move. But all those boxes feel like hiding everything, or dressing in the dark. But she trusts in Randy's decision to move. He takes care of her like that: him leading, her following.

She really doesn't want to move. The old apartment in Cleveland Heights with its oak woodwork and built-in bookshelves with the leaded glass doors is close to her job at Wallgreen's Drugs. They can walk the few blocks to the coffee shop and vintage record shop on Coventry when they want. Randy says people only like change when it is their idea, not somebody else's, but she thinks it's more to it than that. Janine does agree with Randy, though: living in the upstairs of a duplex with the old couple downstairs who own the house, the Fords, is becoming difficult, confrontational, impossible.

"It's not that they're so old that pisses me off," philosophizes Randy, "It's that they are so obnoxious! I don't know about you, but I won't live like this anymore."

Janine's unblinking green eyes look up from the just-packed box of last minute items she has marked as *keepsakes*. Randy is unwinding an extension cord.

She recalls how only a week ago he was looking through the "Unfurnished Apartments for Rent" section of the newspaper. She knows he is methodical, almost rabid, when he's locked on a task like this, so she seals the box with strapping tape and hums tunelessly to herself.

They had barely been in this apartment a week when the banging started. Anytime Randy played a CD—let alone plugging in his Fender Stratocaster—the old folks downstairs would take what must be a broom handle and bang up at their ceiling for the noise to stop.

"It's not like they've got kids or anything," says Randy. "Jeez, even at three in the freaking afternoon they do it when I turn on a radio. I'm a musician, damn it, and I need music. What do they want me to shrivel up and die—like them?" Randy shouts the last two words down at the floor. He stomps his feet: once, twice. Within a minute, a bang comes from below. Then a second one.

"Now Randy," cautions Janine, "maybe there's something we can do, you know, to make it work out."

"Balls!" Randy barks in reply, "Not after the other night when they banged their ceiling because they thought we were making too much noise in our own bed. No, this is war! War!" he says as he stomps—one, two, three. He waits, breathing heavily, until the three bangs he expects are heard.

But Janine is looking at a small plastic box with the two electrical prongs and the numbered dial, a K-Mart timer which Randy has just bought.

"What are you going to do with this?" Janine asks Randy.

"Look around us, Janine," says Randy with a sweep of his hand. "Nothing left to drive over to the new place after this load but this boom box here," he says, patting the black plastic CD player like it's a black plastic dog, "and we can get this tomorrow."

After Randy hooks up the extension cord, he moves the boom box to the center of the room. Then he pulls a *Guns and Roses* CD from his pocket, puts it in, and snaps it shut. His face is a cross between a snarl and a grin.

"Which album is it?" asks Janine.

"Doesn't matter, does it?" he says. "Anything by Axl Rose and the Slash man plays about the same, doesn't it?"

Randy plugs the extension cord into the timer. He spins the dial to set it for 3 A.M., then plugs the thing in the wall.

"And now," says Randy in a grandiose, TV announcer voice, "Ladies and gentlemen, I give you—*Full Volume!*" He makes a flourish of turning up the silent dial. Randy begins imitating a rock guitarist and miming what music videos present as a stereotypical rock singer's facial expressions: somewhere between ecstasy and bad intestinal gas.

Laughing, Randy looks into Janine's green eyes and asks, "Can you imagine? Can you picture what this will be like at three in the morning? The old farts will peck right through the freaking floor!"

"I don't know, Randy," Janine says, "Don't you this this is a bit too much?"

"Opera would be a bit much," he says. He's agitated, starting to pace around the small room. "Definitely no *Madame Butterfly*. I'd try old-style Country and Western, somebody like Buck Owens and the Buckaroos maybe, but they might like that. Perry Como would definitely be some type of cruel and unusual punishment, don't you think? Naw, this is just a little payback, and you know what they say about paybacks, don't you?"

"They're a bitch?" ventures Janine.

"They're earth-ending loud!" says Randy, who laughs loud himself, and is joined by Janine's tiny, breathless laugh.

Randy's smile is wider than the bumper on a moving truck as he locks the deadbolt. He whistles softly "You Can't Always Get What You Want" as he and Janine walk hand-in-hand down the steps to the pickup.

After Randy and Janine get into the truck, they look back at the two-story house divided into two different apartments, holding two different lives. They watch as curtains on the first floor window part, then close again, as if with a sign of relief.

Randy starts the truck and they pull away from the curb. The truck moves into the lane and down the street. The dusking sky is a harsh neon pink, and dark birds wheel in raucous pairs above the horizon.

BABY'S IN BLACK

A dozen hitchhikers spread out along the entrance ramp to the highway west of Grand Junction. They are far enough apart that if a car stops, the driver can let them in and no one else. It's like the hitchhiker is a winner and the driver has picked their number in the ride lottery, taking them to the next game of chance.

Though it's early in the morning, it's already hot, a dry heat, and quiet except for the hum of semi tires on the blacktop. The cloudless sky seems immense, higher and more domed than the Midwest where I'm from. With a landscape this large, it seems like I'm able to see everything that can come at me.

The story I heard when I got to this ramp is that the local sheriff, who doesn't abide by *dirty hippies*, likes to drive up the entrance ramp and harasses the hitchhikers by making everyone pick up their packs and mill around like they were really walking. Then he cuts across the gravel shoulder back onto the exit ramp, driving off in a flurry of sharp stones. I haven't seen this yet, but I've heard about it from the other hitchhikers who speak of this with awe and concern. I expect that when the sheriff shows up, things will get even hotter.

A short time later, a stocky guy in a burgundy tee shirt and a pair of ratty corduroy pants comes up the entrance ramp. With him is a young German shepherd, a red bandana tied around its neck. It trots like an aristocrat, head held high and ears pointed like a tiara. The guy plays fetch with the dog, tossing a stick, keeping the dog occupied.

After another twenty minutes or so, I notice that everybody starts picking up their backpacks. They start milling around, going nowhere. Just moving.

The sheriff's car is coming.

But the stocky kid and his dog stay still, like they're trying to be statues, like they won't be seen if they don't move.

The sheriff drives past them, me, the next two hitchhikers, then slows to a stop. Sits there for a minute or two, his car idling. Then he backs up, past the two hitchhikers, past me, back to the kid and his dog, where he stops. If I was hungry and lived on stress, I'd eat this moment.

When the sheriff gets out of his car, I see that he is small, young. If I had to characterize him in a word, I'd say he seems cocky. If he dressed differently, shorts and a striped tee shirt maybe, he could pass for a fourteen year old. But he has a badge and hitchhiking is illegal, so he can be as big as he wants.

Though I can't hear what they are saying, I can see each of them is talking, articulating, gesturing, the sheriff slowly and deliberately, small jabs of his hands, the hitchhiker wildly and rapidly, with great sweeps of his arms.

It's not my business I tell myself, so I pick up and shoulder my pack and walk along the entrance ramp berm, going toward the highway. I hear a car backfire but I don't look. I don't want to be the trouble or anywhere near the trouble, especially when the trouble wears a badge.

The sheriff's car comes up on me, the sound of tires on small gravel, the low hum of the engine. He slows to my pace, looks at me. I look back at him through the car windows. His eyes hide behind his aviator sunglasses and his Smokey the Bear hat brim casts a shadow over his face. This face-off seems like it lasts an hour. Then he accelerates, turns quickly on the berm of the exit ramp. I turn away from the stones his tires kick up, gravel that stings like a cloud of angry insects.

In the silence that follows the sound of the car's motor droning off into the distance, I hear another sound. A moan. A wail. A howl.

I turn around and see the stocky guy walking off the entrance ramp and back into town. He's carrying the German shepherd in his arms. The dog hangs limp in his arms, its head lolling, the tongue hanging out, the bandana at its neck noticeable from this increasing distance. I think of Lear and Cordelia, of the moment in which their last hope has left. I imagine the moment after.

DAY TRIPPER

The child is as old as her ears and eyes added together. She's as lively as a box of puppies, moody as Ohio weather.

Yesterday she pressed the Cheerios through the colander on the sofa. Today she cooked bacon grease at the stove like her mom who caught her standing on a chair doing it and who said *shitpissdamn*. Then lifted her off the step stool and hugged her until she laughed and cried at the same time.

So I take her to Wade Park, by the museum. When she goes by the lagoon to look at the water lilies, I grab her by the hood and pull her back from several brinks in a blink. I bet she still thinks those flowers were there just for her.

On the way back home to Little Italy, she fogs the window with her breath, uses her finger to write her name, each time the same one letter backwards. The bus driver honks at a driver who cuts him off, so the child yells, *Wake up, you moron!* I think she means the bus driver, but then I realize she means the other driver.

By the time we get home, she's sleepy. She tells her stuffed animals—Aristotle, Socrates, Hippocrates, and Ferdinand—about her day at the lagoon. "They know what I said," she says. And they will, one friend for each ear, each eye.

HELLO, GOODBYE

I

Ethel Crowe loves the sound of the calliope. On this July night in 1912, the twenty-two-year old rides the electric trolley from Cleveland's West Side out to Avon Point Park with James Egan, her beau who is sweet on her. She likes to ride the merry-go-round. Her favorite carved horse, the dappled gray with the black mane and the raised right hoof, prances on the outside position of the four carved wooden horses, far enough away from the calliope for her to hear the sounds of people laughing in the night throughout the rest of the park. She loves this ride even more than the candied apples James Egan will buy her to eat while they listen to the brass band play waltzes in the gazebo.

II

My friends and I wade, our rods and tackle boxes above our heads, around the fences by the intake pumps to fish off the piers back behind the coal-burning electric power plant. Sometime in the nineteen thirties it replaced the old Avon Point park. Fishing is good here where the water is always warmer and the catch always better: white bass, carp, crappie, yellow perch, and the best prize, walleye, though I've seen salmon and even northern pike on occasion taken here. Pfluger sinkers are twenty-nine cents for an eight ounce box and wooden bobbers are eleven cents apiece at the Western Auto store that's two stores past the turn-in side road that leads to "The Cut," the place we like to fish.

III

Ethel laughs, whirling in slow circles, catching glimpses of the sun setting through the magic lantern made by the horses spinning past the light. Carried on the Northwest breezes are the scents of popcorn, pipe tobacco, funnel cakes, perspiration, her own makeup, fried fish, the fresh moist scent of night air. Ignoring the barkers' calls, she hums along with the music box tune of the calliope, looks over at James Egan whose face she has seen many times walking through the green door of the West Side Hibernian Club where her father drinks beer with the other men from the fire station after his shift is up.

IV

Night fishing: the Coleman lantern's mesh wick is on low, the cigarette's tips burning as we inhale, and the stars above Lake Erie are points of fire that make me feel as though the earth and space are one. I learn to be a philosopher while I fish, that doing-nothing that fishing is, and learn to smoke, to blow smoke rings, and to French inhale through my nose. Done fishing, I carry my rod lightly in my right hand and my tackle box in my left hand, walking along the edge of Electric Boulevard, a tar and cinder street built in layers upon the track bed of the old trolley line that used to come all the way out from Cleveland and turn around at the Saddle Inn, the only restaurant and motel at Avon Point. And return back again. At night the power plant's tall smokestacks cough out sparks that sift down to settle like deserting armies of fireflies, or the sparkling confetti that is left over after fireworks have exploded. If the wind off the lake is right, they swirl as if dancing to some unheard music: a brass band, a calliope, or a merry-go-round.

V

Ethel walks with James Egan who holds her hand as lightly as if it is a live minnow he cups in his palm, and they catch the last trolley back to Cleveland's West Side before she breaks the curfew her father has set for her. Her head resting lightly upon James Egan's left shoulder, she looks out of the trolley window. Set against the rows of grapevines in the vineyard, a boy with a fishing rod and a tackle box is walking.

The Continuing Story of Bungalow Bill

"The Lone Ranger and Tonto are riding in the desert one day," I tell my older brother Rick as I start the joke, "and all of a sudden they are being chased by a bunch of Indians."

"What were the Indians doing in the desert?" Rick asks. He's the oldest, the parent-pleaser, gets the good grades in school and likes math. He's pressing Turtle Wax into the finish of Mom's Ford Falcon at the same time as he waters the grass seed Dad has planted in the yard of the new split level we've moved into. Rick has the car radio on, some AM station out of Detroit playing Motown.

"How do I know?" I say, sitting on the cool floor of the attached garage, watching him. "It's just the way the joke goes."

"Uh-huh," he says in that disinterested way an older brother with a driver's license has of answering younger brothers who don't. He's looking at the soaked center of the straw-covered front yard, considering moving the sprinkler to another location closer to the dry area near the driveway where he's working.

"So the Indians chase the Lone Ranger and Tonto until suddenly they realize they are in a dead-end canyon, trapped and done-for," I continue.

"Yeah, then what?" he says, picking up the length of the hose nearest him.

At sixteen, Rick is too cool to walk behind the wet shrubs and turn off the spigot. Instead, he bends the hose he's holding into a loop and crimps it shut, keeping the two hose pieces tight in his left hand. The just-gurgling sprinkler is pulled toward him with his right hand until he can pick it up.

He takes about four steps into the front yard until the ground turns wet, soft, so he sets the sprinkler down, walks back to the driveway, and releases the crimp in the hose. The water leaps like a fountain from the sprinkler, a surge of pent-up water pressure, then settles down to a gentle sprinkle.

"So the Lone Ranger turns to Tonto," I tell my brother, now that I have his attention again, "and asks, 'What do we do now, Tonto?'" I'm wandering out to the tall pin oak near the curb, looking down for acorns to toss across the street. "And you know what Tonto says?"

But my brother isn't listening to me. He's just realized that the water from the now too-close sprinkler is landing on the car he's waxing. I'm surprised as, instead of crimping the hose again to move the sprinkler, he jumps into the car, turns the key he's left in the ignition, and, *vroom*, he pulls the car quickly into the garage, jumps from the car, and runs out to move the hose. This time he goes behind the wet shrubs to turn it off at the spigot.

As the *tlickita-tlickita* sound of the sprinkler stops, we both hear it at the same time: *rurra-rurra-rurra*, the sound of a motor struggling, of tires spinning. When he jumped from the car to move the hose, he never took the car out of gear, so the little blue Falcon is nosed up against the back wall of the garage, pushing the wall a foot off its base, trying to bull its way into the family room on the other side. I'm laughing, a nervous release, the pitch of my laughter rising to match the decibel level of the car's racing engine.

Rick yells as he runs to the Falcon, jumps in, throws the automatic drive into reverse, and floors the accelerator, *vroooom*, to get the car off the back wall and out of the garage. Only, in his panic, his desire for quick resolution, he forgets to close the driver's side door so, as the car shoots out of the garage, its open door catches the handle of Mom's new freezer on the left wall of the garage: the car door is pulled, *screetch-awk*, all the way around, nearly ripped off, and slammed *bang* into the left front panel above the wheel well; the freezer door caves in, *choonk*, like a sink-hole, the seals around the edges busting, the frost escaping into the warm August afternoon like smoke lingering after a fire. Because the car is going nearly twenty-five miles an hour in reverse, Rick brakes hard, *arr-errrk*, making a ten-foot long skid mark the color of black ash on the driveway.

My brother sits in the Falcon, shaking, as pale as a brand-new white-wall tire. As though in a trance, he inches the car slowly back into the garage. Then he closes the garage door as quietly as he can.

I've decided I'm not going to stick around. I'm going to go to the park down the street, or maybe over to one of my friends' houses, maybe ride my bike to Mayor's Park on the lake, anywhere but here. It's only a matter of time before our parents come home, and I know how Dad gets when he's mad.

"Oh my God," my brother moans, "What do we do now?"

"What do you mean *we*, pale-face?" I say and grin.

Nowhere Man

When Otto Porter leased the second floor sleeping room in Elsie Mueller's house, she knew she had found a good thing. He wasn't like that hooligan her neighbor Mrs. Coyne rented a room in her attic to, a foul-mouthed Great Lakes sailor who was usually drunk on the six days a month he slept there on leave. Elsie's boarder's rent was paid on time, his room was tidy, his manners refined, and his comings-and-goings quiet and considerate. He took the trash out to the alley all on his own and he cut the grass with the reel mower because he liked to be out-of-doors, he said, days when the weather was inviting.

Though the skeleton key opened both the front door and the kitchen door at the back of the brick four-square, Mr. Porter used it only on the side door. Entry into the parlor, he'd told her, was unthinkable and passing through the kitchen seemed intrusive. He found the side entrance into the hallway with its access to the back staircase leading to his room more suitable.

Although the room was small, Otto felt comfortable. The iron framed single bed nestled against the wall wasn't a divan, but with two pillows to bolster him, it provided an extra place to sit. The oak dresser with its beveled mirror was adequate for his clothes, and the closet held his two suits and his overcoat and raincoat while its upper shelf were adequate for his fedoras. Centered in the west-facing window was an armchair with a footstool where he liked to sit and read in the sunlight on weekend afternoons.

In many ways, Elsie thought, but didn't tell Mrs. Coyne, her boarder was easier to live with than her children were or her deceased husband had been.

*   *   *

Elsie's husband, Conrad, worked for thirty-one years on the assembly line at the Fisher Body Plant on Brookpark Road near the airport. He built Chevrolets. A slight man, he was taciturn and reticent. On occasion he was known to say a few words from behind the newspaper that was like a folding screen partitioning him from the world. Praise was not his strong suit.

For Conrad's fiftieth birthday, Elsie spent two days preparing his favorite meal of roasted stuffed capon, mashed potatoes and gravy, string beans, and apple pie with vanilla ice cream for dessert. She watched him fork the meal with mechanical precision into his mouth. When she finally asked how he liked the birthday dinner, he replied, "I'm eating it, ain't I"?

Elsie noticed how his slight figure grew a paunch after years of eating his morning meal of two eggs fried in the grease from four crisp rashers of bacon, served with thickly buttered and marmaladed toast. One morning, a few weeks after his birthday, Conrad was swinging open the garage door to pull out his Chevy so he could drive to work when his arteries closed up tight and he fell to the cinder floor, dead from a heart attack.

Elsie's grown children, Tom, a nail salesman who had just moved his young wife, daughter and son to the western suburbs, and Terry, who was attending Ohio State on the GI Bill to take a degree in chemical engineering, suggested she take in a boarder so that she wouldn't have to live alone. The ad for the "Room to Let" which Terry had written, paid for and placed himself, was the one Elsie's boarder found the two days later in *The Cleveland Press*.

In the unseasonably cold and drizzly autumn of 1954, Otto Porter was told by his wife's doctor that the high humidity and the off-lake dampness of Cleveland's winter would only speed his wife Flossie's demise from tuberculosis. She was fifty-three, he two years her senior. To provide the best care possible for her regardless of cost, Mr. Porter would have to sell their brick bungalow in Lakewood to pay for Flossie to stay in an Arizona sanitarium where she could be properly treated. Since his position as an accountant with the Cleveland Trolley Line was secure and paid reasonably well, he had no choice but to remain in Ohio and visit her twice a year or more by train.

In October some months later, Otto sat on the train returning from his second visit to Arizona. Looking out the dining car window, he saw the dry Southwest landscape blur as the train raced into the night. In the morning, he would see the harvested fields of the Midwest quilting the terrain as if in preparation for the long winter sleep. When he arrived at Elsie Mueller's house, a telegram was waiting for him. Flossie had died in her sleep the night he left.

Otto borrowed against the money he expected from the sale of their home to bring his wife back to Ohio for burial, as she'd wished. The following week, Otto's supervisor at the Cleveland Trolley Line called him into his office. Unable to compete with the explosion of automobiles that were now everywhere, he said, the company had to cut the fat from its payroll in order to survive. His supervisor laid Otto off. Two weeks later, Otto rode the trolley to his new job at the Koepke Meat Processing Company where he worked at a reduced income as a payroll clerk. With the transaction about to close on his house, Otto needed to make arrangements, so he opened his morning copy of *The Plain Dealer* to the "Sleeping Rooms" section as the trolley clanged along Clifton Boulevard toward the Cuyahoga River, then downtown Cleveland, where he'd transfer to the bus that took him to his new job.

Elsie was only too happy to tell her son Tom she could watch the children so that his wife Fran could accompany him to the trade show in Chicago; Friday morning through Monday evening would be fine. Elsie loved having Alice and little Tommy visit, especially on Sundays, and the thought of four whole days filled her with delight.

On Saturday morning she would pull the children in a wagon the four blocks to the Sears and Roebuck store where she'd get the children new outfits for Sunday mass. They bought fresh-ground peanut butter and crisp apples from Mr. Marzitti, the green grocer in the small market attached by a walkway to Sears. On Saturday night, there'd be popcorn and root beer floats for the children as they listened to the radio or watched one of the television variety shows. And on Sunday morning, Alice and little Tommy, freshly-scrubbed, clothes ironed and shoes polished, would accompany her to church at Saint Ignatius Loyola Cathedral where all her neighbors—the Catholic ones at any rate—would see how lovely her grandchildren were, how well-dressed and well-behaved.

Elsie planned to bake an apple pie and two loaves of bread, then roast a stuffed chicken on Sunday for dinner. She could picture Alice reading the Sunday funnies to little Tommy at the kitchen table while she made the gravy.

The girl, about seven years of age with curly mousy-brown hair and a slight overbite, pulled her four-year-old brother, a thin child with cow-licked hair, by the hand until they stood next to the claw foot iron tub.

"This is the bathtub," Alice told little Tommy.

Tommy leaned over to look into the tub. The scent of Ivory soap and bleach made him feel like he's going to sneeze.

"And this is the sink, "Alice announced ceremonially. "Watch," she commanded, as she stepped up on the small step stool so that her short arms could reach the handles, marked H and C, of the pedestal sink.

"Where's the under?" the boy asked.

"Oh, like the cabinet?" Alice asked. "Granma's old bathroom doesn't have one. It's all on this stand. And that's why the stool is here. So you can stand," Alice professed. "Now you try," she said.

She stepped down and then lifted the boy on to the stool. His chin was on the edge of the porcelain sink. He could see the handles, but he couldn't reach them.

"Tommy," Alice said, in her best mommy-voice, "You be sure to wash your hands before and after every meal!"

"Alice! Tommy!" Elsie called from the front parlor, "Come down for hot cocoa!"

"We are," said Alice. Then she lifted her brother down from the stool and, taking him by the hand, led him from the bathroom out into the hallway. Just before the landing where they would hold the railing to go down, Alice stopped in front Mr. Porter's room, with its closed maple door and a glass handle.

"And Tommy," Alice whispered, excited by sharing a secret, "this is where grandma's boarder lives!"

Otto Porter had spent a pleasant afternoon at the downtown library. He'd read about Hemingway's latest safari in *Life* magazine, followed by an hour reading a few passages from the new volume of Sandburg's *Lincoln*. Around four o'clock in the afternoon, after a fried egg sandwich at Pete's Westside Diner, he returned to Elsie's house, the Sandburg under his arm, to settle in and read in the armchair while the light from the window was still good.

When he stopped into the bathroom just across and down the hall from his room, he found a small, thin boy—ruddy-cheeked, dark cow-licked hair, about four or five years old—standing on the small stool in front of the sink. The boy wasn't doing anything, just standing and looking at the faucet as though it might provide water merely by his wishing so.

"Hello," Otto said.

The boy looked to him, held his gaze, then looked back at the faucet.

"Do you need some help?" Otto asked the boy.

The boy nodded his head yes.

"Well, what?" asked the man.

The boy pointed at the faucet.

Otto stepped close to the sink, turning the hot and cold handles, adjusting them for lukewarm, a temperature he believed would be suitable for the boy.

"There you are, then," he said.

The boy stared at the water coming out of the faucet.

Stepping back, Otto looked at the boy at the sink, asking, "Can you reach the water?"

The boy nodded and lifted himself onto his toes, resting his belly on the rim of the sink. He shook his hands around in the water, then announced, "Done!"

Otto took a small blue towel from the bar next to the tub and handed it to the boy who waited on the stool. The boy shook his hands in the towel in a manner very similar to the way he had done with the water.

"Done," he said, handing the towel to the man.

Otto laid it over the side of the tub.

"Are you Tommy, Elsie's grandson?" Otto asked.

The boy blinked but said nothing.

"OK," Otto said, "Tell you what: if you are Tommy, say nothing. Or blink. Either one so I know who you are."

The boy blinked and said nothing.

"All right, then," Otto said more to himself than to the boy, "This all adds up now." He sat on the edge of the porcelain tub next to the small blue towel, crossed his arms, and studied the boy.

Tommy stepped down from the stool and sat down on it, crossing his arms as if in imitation of the man. "Who are you?" the boy asked.

"I'm Mr. Porter, the boarder," he replied. Then he chuckled, adding, "Doesn't that sound funny, like a rhyme? You know, Porter the boarder?"

The boy said nothing, just watched and blinked.

"Hey," Porter said, "Hey—want to see a magic trick?"

Tommy smiled and clapped his hands twice.

Porter took a buffalo head nickel from his waist coat pocket and held the nickel up between the index finger and thumb of his left hand. As his right hand wrapped around it, seeming to sweep it out of his grip, Porter let the coin drop into the palm of his left hand, which he swung down to his side as he swept his empty, closed right hand up to his lips, then blew air from his mouth loudly into his fist so that it opened, showing an empty hand.

"Where did it go?" he asked Tommy. The boy shook his head from side to side. His mouth was open. His eyes were the size of quarters.

"Maybe," Porter said, reaching his left hand up near the right side of the boy's head, "It's right here in your ear!" And as he said this, he lightly touched Tommy's right ear, brought his left hand down in front of the boy, and opened his hand. There it was, the buffalo head nickel.

Tommy stared at Porter, his eyes the size of silver dollars. "How?" he asked, but Porter put his right finger to his lips and made the *Shhh* gesture. Porter looked left, right, then got up, walked to the door, and looked in both directions down the hallway. "Right," he said, and returned to the edge of the tub where he knew the boy would be waiting for him.

As if to tell a secret, Porter leaned forward. So did Tommy, so he could hear.

"It's a magic nickel," Porter said. "Now hold out your hand," he told the boy, who did as he was told. Then the man put the nickel into the boy's hand and closed it with his own hand around the coin.

"Don't lose it," he said, "Guard it. Can you do that?"

Tommy nodded twice.

"OK then, put it in your pocket where it'll be safe."

"Tommy," came a voice called from downstairs, Elsie's voice, "Come to dinner, Tommy!"

"You'd better go, then," Porter said.

"Coming," Tommy said to the hallway.

Mr. Porter walked with Tommy out into the hallway. As he passed through the doorway, he pulled the string to turn off the light over the mirror.

Tommy stopped in front of Porter's door that was just before the staircase leading downstairs. He looked at Mr. Porter, then curled his right index finger on his right hand in, twice, calling Porter down to him. The man leaned down, bent at the waist, and put his ear near the boy's mouth.

"Be careful," the boy said.

"Why?" asked Porter.

Tommy pointed at Porter's closed door.

"'Cause the hotdog man lives in there!" he warned.

"Who's that," asked Porter, "And why's he called that?"

"I don't know," the boy replied as he turned toward the staircase, "but Granma says he smells like hot dogs."

Otto Porter sat in the side chair next to the window. The Sandburg book sat on the table next to him, a trolley transfer marking the passage he'd read maybe half a dozen times without comprehending. If he opened his door, even a little bit, he would be able to hear the talk and laughter of Elsie and her grandchildren at the dinner table. He kept his door closed.

The golden afternoon light was growing dim. He felt the air coming through the slightly open window turning colder, so he closed the window all the way and pulled his cardigan sweater closer and crossed his arms across his chest, holding his hands under his arms. His head dropped until his chin brushed his sweater. His breathing was deep, with a slight catch as he drew air in. He put his right hand on his forehead, holding it as if the weight was such that he couldn't hold it much longer.

When he looked up, the room was dark. He leaned back in his chair, put his hands on the arms of the chair and gripped the chair tight. Once, years back, when Flossie was young and healthy, she'd talked him into riding a Ferris wheel at the amusement park at Avon Point. He'd sat like this, gripping with his hands, holding on tight. Flossie, laughing, put her hands over his and gave them a squeeze. Closing his eyes, it was as if he could feel her hands on his. How he wished he could! He felt himself grow so light-headed that he could hardly breathe.

Mr. Porter opened his eyes. The room was nearly pitch-dark, with only a faint light coming under the door and through the window. He was gripping the chair so hard his forearms ached. He unclasped his arms, raising his right hand to his mouth. That evening years back on the Ferris wheel he wasn't sure if he was afraid that the ride would start or that it wouldn't. He wasn't sure of anything anymore.

His right hand had formed a fist that he pressed against his lips. He blew air from his mouth into the space between his fingers. *Where did it go?* he said to himself. He didn't need the dark or the light to show him his hand was empty.

HER MAJESTY

This is my apartment, not theirs. Sure, I pay them rent. But I live here in Parma now in this one bedroom apartment that is so much easier for me than my colonial in Brunswick. Two years now I've lived here and it's as good as mine.

Who was it had this carpet put down? Who was it had this wallpaper put up? And what do they give me in return? They raise my rent. Raise my rent!

Not to mention that arrogant young man upstairs—what's his name? Joey? John?—won't walk on the sidewalk, though that's what God put it there on the ground for. No, he's got to walk out the back door and go across my patio. My patio!

Who was it planted the pretty flowers there that bloom in the spring?

Who had the bird feeder put up that attracts the bright birds on the winter days?

And that arrogant young man upstairs—what's his name? Jack? Jimmy?—walks across my patio. He might just as well be walking through my living room as walking across my patio! I just can't go on living like this anymore.

I've called and called the rental agent—what's his name? Tony? Toby?—about having some decent grass planted out there. I told them I needed something green to look at in the summer. They tell me that it is just a back yard here at the apartment complex. But I live on this side of the building, so it is my front yard!

Go on and ask the couple next door—what's their names? Albers? Akers?—they agree with me. Go on, just ask them. They'll tell you.

It wasn't so bad when I still had my little Maisie. Such a sweet little tabby cat. My only friend. When the rental agency—what's it called? Johnson Realty? Jackson Realty?—found out I had her, they made me get rid of her.

Why, I ask? She never scratched the woodwork. She was a clean cat, always used her little box. Who was it that kept her inside where she was safe? Who was it emptied her litter box and cleaned up after her? But they made me get rid of her.

I told them that this apartment was as good as mine and Maisie was my cat and she was staying! Now my niece has her over in Parma Heights. It breaks my heart to go over and see my Maisie there, so I don't go.

My doctor—what's his name? Bagachandra? Chandrabaga? Chagabanderara? Well, at least I can understand him when he talks. And my social worker—what's her name? Sandy? Cindy?—, they both wrote letters telling Jonestone Realty that a cat could help me calm down faster. My little Maisie, my little medicine!

But the agency said no, it's not in the lease, that I shouldn't have had her here in the first place. Mean, that's what they are, just plain mean. She was a clean cat.

I tell you, I can't go on living like this anymore. Not without my little cat—what's her name? Maisie? Daisy? Ditzi?

MAXWELL'S SILVER HAMMER

Jack Needham walks in the door of the boxy blue bungalow on Tupelo Drive and hears a tea kettle whistling on the stove. He picks the kettle up by its hot handle and sets it quickly on another burner; the water nearly boiled off, and the kettle itself hot enough to glow red, like a one-eyed jack-o-lantern in the dark. His wife Jenna must be in the garage, preoccupied with her ceramic art "project" again.

Jack systematically scouts each room of the house as a general course of action, certain he will eventually find Jenna, as he expects he will, in the garage-turned workshop. Even though it's dinnertime in the height of daylight savings time, he can see that the light is on in the garage. Grabbing a cold beer out of the refrigerator, Jack pops the tab, takes a long drink to wash the taste of the metal fabricating plant where he works out of his mouth. As he heads out the back door, he feels his blood heat, simmer, get ready to boil, as it always does, when he remembers how the garage had once been his territory in this marriage. Band saw, router, wood lathe, half completed chairs and shelves: all are pushed to the one side of the garage, making way for Jenna's ceramics. Jack feels distressed, distanced, dispossessed. He stops at the garage window and peers in.

Jenna, wearing cut off denim overalls, brown hair French braided and sticking out of her Cleveland Indians Baseball cap, is busy painting gold trim paint on a three and a half foot high ceramic Elvis, the only one of its kind in the workshop. Elvis' sideburns look like little black caterpillars crawling down the cheeks of an eternally young Elvis, the boy King of Rock and Roll.

Lined up in front of Elvis are the heads of two dozen foot-and a half gnomes all in a row; in front of them are a dozen brown rabbits sitting on their haunches. One of Jenna's favorite words these days is *symmetry*.

"What's for supper tonight, Hon?" Jack asks as he walks in the side door of the garage.

"Whatever you want, darlin'," Jenna replies without looking up, "So long as you catch it and cook it."

"Jeez, Jenna, I'm pizza-ed and fast food burger-ed out," Jack says. "I would eat anything made by your hand. Honest."

Jenna stands stock still, stares at Jack with the look on her face that people have when a name is on the tip of their tongue but they can't quite remember it.

"Eat one of these gnomes," she says with a quick, watery laugh, "I made lots of them."

Jack pulls long on his beer, looking at her side eyed as he does so. He holds the cold can against his forehead, then brings it to his mouth. He swallows his long drink in a series of short gulps that make his Adam's apple jerk up and down like a jack handle, then sets down his can of beer.

"All I know is I never planned on no liquid diet like this," he says as he walks out the garage door.

Jenna hesitates, knows her husband hopes for a reply. She doesn't give him one.

While she is adding more paint to Elvis' collar, she hears the back door of the house slam. Something ceramic smashes.

She pauses, squeezes the paintbrush in her left hand until her knuckles white. Then she adds more paint. She hums a few notes from the beginning of *Love Me Tender.*

Jack opens the second shoebox of the three on the table in front of him. Each one is filled with rubber banded and marked baseball cards. This box holds the Yankees and the Indians. Each card feels like a cardboard shard of history in his hands.

His first ball cards he bought with money from his paper route. He loved the feel of holding each player's greatness in his hands. The other paperboys would trade cards with him while they were all waiting on the corner for their bundles of papers to get delivered from the newspaper delivery truck. Closing his eyes, Jack still hears the litany of The Trade: *Got 'em, got 'em, need 'em, got 'em, triples, need 'em.*

As he showers later, Jack thinks how, as he allows the cards to flow through his hands, it is like he is dealing time. It's like he's constructing a pathway made of cards he can walk on, take him back to his younger days, arriving again at a place where he can trade what he has become in life with what he wished back then he could be now. His new litany is *Need 'em, need 'em, need 'em."*

When he comes out of the off-mauve bathroom looking for another cold beer to drink while he finishes dressing, he looks at the kitchen table. It is clear, empty, the shoeboxes gone.

So is Jenna's pale green Plymouth Fury from the driveway.

Florida. To her sister's. The one who always points out to Jenna how much happier her life is since she got divorced. How much better off she is without the cheating, gambling, bullshitting man she was married to. That's where she has gone, Jack tells himself. He holds another cold beer to his head where his left temple throbs.

In his mind he pictures Jenna driving down towards West Virginia on 77 South, tossing baseball cards one by one out the window, watching them twist like leaves in the air. *Die, sucker!* he can hear her say. And the names roll off of his tongue also one by one: Micky Mantle, Tito Francona, Harmon Killibrew, Roger Maris, Bob Feller, Rocky Calovito, Early Wynn. Gone, gone, his pathway back to his paperboy youth gone.

In the garage turned workshop, Jack locates his twelve-pound sledge in a corner near his wood lathe. Because the gnomes are so small, so low to the ground, he swings the sledge as if it were a driving iron; he keeps his head down, follows through. He loves the sound of the ceramic pinging as the gnome shards shatter against the wall.

Before he goes at the bunnies, he pops the tab on another beer. Jack decides to set the bunnies on the ceramic Elvis's head after he finds an old Louisville Slugger up on the wall by the snow shovels. He's grinning like a nine-year old kid playing tee-ball.

"Batter up!" he calls as he sets the bat on his shoulder.

The phone is ringing when Jack walks in the back door of the blue bungalow on Tupelo Drive. He grabs the last beer from the fridge with his left hand as he picks up the phone with his right. The phone feels like a dead cat in his hand.

"'Lo?" he says.

"It's me," says Jenna.

"Where are you?" Jack says.

"Where do you think?" Jenna taunts.

"Marietta?" he says.

"And just why would I want to be in Marietta, anyway?"

"I thought maybe you were on your way to your sister's in Florida," says Jack, feeling heavy with alcohol, sheepish with embarrassment.

"Don't be such an ass, Jack," she says. "I'm at mom's. I just wanted to get away for a while. Sometimes we need to do that, you know?"

"Listen, Jenna, are my ball cards all gone?" Jack says into the telephone.

"I put them under the bed, with your shoes," she says. "I just want to keep you on your toes." The she adds: "That's a joke, Jack, so laugh whenever it hits you."

Jack lets the air out of his lungs as though he's a car tire with a large puncture.

"I just need you to notice me more, Jack, that's all," Jenna says.

Jack is looking out the window at the sun setting.

"So I'll be home in a while and maybe I'll make us something to eat, OK? And you can watch the ballgame on TV after that and I'll work a little more on my Elvis to unwind. And then, maybe we can cuddle on the couch and watch the news like we used to do, before bed. I'd like that. I'd like that a lot. Wouldn't you, Jack?"

Jack is still looking out the window. His eyes hurt. He squints hard at the red sun.

Penny Lane

Right after religion and just before history, Sister Scholastica lines up our sixth grade class and takes us outside. The fall afternoon is warm and leaves fall from the trees out of sheer excitement.

Quietly the first and second graders stand, hands at their sides. One girl has a chapel cap bobby pinned to her hair. The older kids, the seventh and eighth graders, are bouncy, pushy, talking as the nuns lead their classes out to gather along the street. On a normal day, we're not supposed to be within fifty feet of the street without getting a detention.

Sister has the class follow her about halfway between the three elm trees where I had fought and lost my first fistfight with Lenny Armbruster just two weeks before and the O'Daley's garage just off the church property, behind which I had kissed Katie Cassidy just three weeks before, this leading to my fight with Lenny Armbruster, my mouth amazed in both cases.

Like party lights we string along the road on the frontage of the church property on Lake Road, all six hundred and fifty seven of us—eight grades, eleven nuns, four lay teachers, the parish priest Father Zimmer, and even Mrs. Mitchell the secretary, whose husband Tugboat owns Del's boat rental where I buy minnows on Saturday mornings when I fish off the pier near Avon Point.

Soon the buzzing began: *He's coming! There's the car! Is it him? Who's that with him? He's here! I see him!*

From the corner of my eye I see Sister Scholastica and Sister Euphrasia, Sister John Bosco and Sister Mary Margaret Clare, tears dripping from their eyes like wax from altar candles. One by one they lift the crucifixes from the rosaries they use for belts, kissing the large wooden crosses as if they are lovers just returned from a long trip among the heathens.

When I look up, I see him.

John Fitzgerald Kennedy, the Catholic presidential candidate, riding in a large white open convertible, driving down Lake Road, the road which runs from Cleveland to Lorain, campaigning for votes in Ohio. Kids are chanting K-E-N-N-E-D-Y and tossing handfuls of pale grass in the air as if it is confetti or green fireworks.

As Kennedy's motorcade slows down, he lifts himself up out of the seat and onto the boot where the convertible top has been folded down. Sitting there like an uncrowned prince, elevated, waving, smiling, basking, he looks just like he does on television, just like he does on the cover of *Life* magazine. My small life enters history for the briefest moment, as if a lone Roman candle has gone off, one bright burst of sound and light and significance.

Then he is gone.

Gone, shot dead in the late fall only four years later in another open convertible, slumped over this time, Jackie crawling out onto the boot, images which overlay the first image so that the two seem forever linked, conjoined, inextricable. That second burst of sound like another Roman candle, another flash of light tearing a hole in the fabric of my childhood, the air escaping like a whisper, a hush, a prayer, the sound votive candles make as they flicker out, leaving the church in utter silence.

The White Album

A man wakes to a wave of silence. It spreads out on his bed like a new coat. He tries it on and likes the fit—a little long at the wrists, but it doesn't choke him at the collar. He likes the way the fit made him feel. He hangs it on a hook on the back of the closet door and goes downstairs to breakfast.

Sitting at the table, eating Cream of Wheat and reading the entertainment section is a mime dressed as a white dove. The man is unsure whether he is looking at his clone, his twin, someone on a day pass from the local institution, or an apprentice Emmett Kelly from the old school of clowning.

Instead of asking for clarification, the man decides to go outside and launch his new kite. On some previous day, he constructed the kite from a kit which only he had imagined, made from linen handkerchiefs, mother's milk, and cirrocumulus clouds: he can not remember the date or the day of the week, but he is certain of the month: May. He watches the beige geometric construction float and dart, dance with the wind, swing and dip. By listening closely, he hears the sound the kite makes as it slices air: *swish, swoosh, swish*. Once the kite cut off more breeze than could sustain its flight, it zigs down and crashes.

The sound of the kite breaking acted like a starting gun for every electric and motor-driven appliance on the block, creating an orchestrated cacophony of riding lawn mowers, sunbeam mixers, weed whackers, paint strippers, radios, security system checkers, pet zappers, cell phones, and vibrating patio furniture.

So back goes the man into his house and climbs quietly the stairs. It seems certain to him that someone or something had clandestinely let the air out of him. He puts the wave of silence back on, rakishly putting up the collar, and hooks his thumbs in the pockets. *This helps,* he thinks, *now I'm in balance,* picturing himself with his feet strapped to the top of a 1920's bi-plane in a loop-de-loop flying circus, hearing the air go by his ears: *swish, swoosh.*

The twin headphones for his white IPhone fit his head like a stocking cap made out of baby's breath. It seems to him as though the thin cord connecting the headphones to the IPhone must look a little like kite string.

GOOD DAY SUNSHINE

The rent was due when the electric company sent a letter telling me they were going to cut my power off for late payments. I could stand being broke in the daylight, but not in the dark. I'd been out of work since the economy collapsed and crushed my job. Since I couldn't sit still in my apartment another minute waiting for the landlord to knock on the door, I went out looking for work on a Friday afternoon, the time slot where job applications go to die.

The industrial park was gray warehouses and assembly plants that looked like packing crates or shipping boxes. The buildings, set close to the street, had thin strips of grass and trimmed shrubs that looked artificial. Along the paved sidewalks were cigarette butts, candy wrappers, plastic bags, Styrofoam cups. A scrap of paper caught my eye. A bright red half-page with gold letters, it read *Give Jesus a High Five and Look Up to the Lord for Help.* So I looked up and no bull, right in front of me, at eye-level like I was about to walk into it, was a sign that read *Help Wanted.* "Well holy hell," I said.

I examined the flat-roofed, metal-sided building that looked exactly like all the others in the industrial park, wondering what kind of company this was and what they made. There was a large black and white sign that said *Yes: An International Corporation.* "OK," I said, "Let's find out what this is all about." So I opened the heavy metal door and stepped in.

It was dark until my eyes adjusted to the dim light. I walked up a long flight of stairs to the door at the top of the landing. I could smell metal, oil, cardboard, rubber. The door, oak planks with aged metal clasps and knobs, didn't belong here; it belonged on the front of a house in a rich neighborhood, or on one of the old churches downtown. I knocked, but the wood was so heavy it absorbed the sound my knuckles made, so I had to pound the door with my fist.

I waited. Nothing. I pounded again.

Just as I was starting to turn to walk back down the staircase and leave, the door opened, slowly, and I was face to face with a tiny woman with gray hair pulled into a bun, horn-rimmed glasses, a blue polyester suit, sensible shoes, and one of those old-fashioned watches pinned to her jacket. She was surely somebody's grandmother. She must have come with the door, I thought.

"Go right on in," she said, smiling and pointing to the open door on the other side of what was obviously her office. "He's expecting you."

Who's *he?* I wondered as I crossed to the door.

When I went in, the light was so bright I winced, flinched, turned my head away. I squinted as I looked up. What seemed like half a dozen desk lamps were on, as well as the fluorescent ceiling lights. The furniture was glossy white and chrome, from the huge desk in front of the sunlit window to the chairs and bookshelves. The room was as bright as a TV set, as a photo shoot, stuff I'd seen in movies.

"Bill," a calm voice said, "Welcome. Come in and have a seat. We've been waiting for you."

I turned toward the man who said this, the man who knew my name without his asking or my telling. He was over six feet tall, clean-shaven, with cropped silver hair. He wore a cream-colored double-breasted suit with a light gray tie. The light glinted off his glasses like they were mirrors. But they were not, I could see that. And I could see that no matter which way he turned his head, the light glinted—no, it came out of his eyeglasses—to meet my gaze. It was like I was in one of those old black and white movies where some hardass detective shines a powerful beam of light into a poor guy's face, asking him where he was on the night of the twenty-third at nine o'clock or something.

The man put out his hand. His handshake was hot, but his body gave off a coolness like when the refrigerator door is open. He pointed to a chair in front of his desk, and as I sat down he sat on the desk.

"Bill," he asked, "what's your take on the contemporary split between the public and the private life?"

My mouth moved for a few seconds like I was chewing up my answer into small pieces so I could spit it out. Then I said, "In private, we're all equal, rich or poor. But only the rich have public lives."

He tossed his head back and laughed so that his mouth was open and even though I could see the light being squeezed from the corners of his eyes, I imagined I could see light emanating from the silver fillings in his teeth.

"That's rich!" he said. I thought he meant it was funny, but I wasn't certain he didn't mean he disagreed.

"Let me ask you this, then," he said, "to whom should a man be loyal?"

I wasn't sure how to answer. So many people had been disloyal to me: my mother who went to the store for milk when I was thirteen and never came back; my old man who kicked me out when I was fifteen because I didn't want be the baseball player he never was; the woman I loved when I was twenty-two and who loved me so much that she left me for my best friend Eddie who had run off with me when I got kicked out. The pool of possible answers was shrinking like a splash of water on a summer sidewalk.

"A dog," I said, thinking of the hound mix I found on the side of the road when I was fifteen and hitchhiking and that I had until I was twenty-two when the woman I had loved and my ex-best friend traded the dog for a bottle of tequila. "You can tell a dog anything and it will keep your secrets."

"Ah, but isn't that because the dog can't talk?" the man said quizzically.

"That's the beauty of the thing," I replied, crossing my left leg over my right.

The man with the illuminated glasses clapped his hands, not like in applause for what I said, but the way little kids do when something pleases them.

"OK, just one more," he said.

"Third's the charm, my grandmother used to say," I said.

"Can you keep a secret?" he asked.

"Sure can," I said, looking him in the eyes.

"Good, very good," the man said. He returned to a chair behind the desk and started to look at some papers that were spread on the desktop.

I waited about a minute.

"You going to tell me the secret I'm supposed to keep?" I asked.

"No need," he said, looking up. "I just wanted to know that if I had to give you a secret, I could. I probably won't. But it's a good thing to know, isn't it?"

I nodded my head like I knew what he meant but I was nodding to myself that yes, this was weird and I didn't really get it.

"That's it then," he said, standing. "You're our man. You've got the job. We'd like you to start first thing on Monday morning."

He put out his hand to me again. I stood too, put my hand out and we shook. His hand was as soft as a kid glove, as firm as a bank counter.

"Great," I replied, "Great. Only," I asked with a small laugh, "Just what exactly *is* this position you've just hired me for?"

He lifted his face toward the ceiling lights and laughed loudly, his mouth open, his even white teeth catching the florescent glint. Then he brought his eyes level to mine so that I could see the red rims of his blue eyes through the silver frames of his glasses. His right hand reached out and he patted me twice on the shoulder, then left the hand there.

"Bill," he said, "a company like ours needs a sense of humor like yours, really. Laughter in the face of adversity—*that's* the key," he said, with a wink, *"that's* the *key!"*

"Now I have to let you go," he told me, steering me toward the door. "My next appointment is due any minute. My secretary will show you out. But we'll see you Monday morning, bright and early, ready to start work, right?"

"Right you are, Sir," I replied, almost snapping to attention.

He guided my by the elbow to the door, opening it so I could pass through the outer office and go down the long staircase to the street. "Monday, then," he said, looking at me, his smile a radiance that ignited the room.

Outside again, it was growing cold. I should have felt good, being hired and having work again, but it didn't feel that way. The clean lines of the manufacturing plants were becoming obscured as the long shadows of late afternoon stretched into the growing evening. Night was coming. Though I couldn't see them yet, I bet there were stars in the sky.

I turned back to look at the building. The room where I'd been interviewed was still bright, light coming out of the two windows that looked like luminous eyes or illuminated screens waiting for a movie to begin. Then, as if a switch had been turned off or a candle snuffed, the window lights were suddenly extinguished and I was left in the dark.

Paperback Writer

He said, "Your son is not working up to his potential."

She said, "How do you know that?"

He said, "If you could see the intelligence tests and achievement tests he has completed, you would not accept the marks he's getting in this class."

She said, "I know he can do better. I believe the next six weeks will prove it."

He said, "Your son's effort has surely slackened and is reflected in his current grades."

She said, "He likes to read."

He said, "Although bright and a top reader, he seems distracted, misdirected."

She said, "I guess his nose is always buried in the wrong book."

He said, "His scores suffer because he doesn't seem to check his work before turning it in."

She said, "There are times when he refuses to do a homework assignment, then reconsiders and goes ahead and does it."

He said, "He's a nonconformist *par excellence*. No matter what he is told to do, he comes up with the annoying habit of offering a substitute he believes is just as good."

She said, "A little nonconformity is good, but maybe his is too much?"

He said, "He is listening harder and his attitude seems better, so I'm still hoping for improvement."

She said, "He daydreams. A lot."

He said, "His daydreaming has become chronic."

She said, "I'll talk with my son and encourage him from my end."

He said, "Good. I think we are no doubt mutually concerned about the kind of career your son might find in the future."

She said, "Oh, he wants to be a writer."

SHE SAID SHE SAID

Rita leans back against the front of the stove, her left arm across her chest and tucked into her right armpit while her right hand holds a can of Pepsi as if it's a weapon she's aiming at someone. Right now, that someone is Troy.

Troy is drinking coffee. He sits in the built-in nook in the dim kitchenette with its small window. Hunched over the folded page of the newspaper, he's reading the baseball scores on the sports page.

"Something's going on here," Rita says to Troy, "and I can feel it." Her voice drops, low and serious. "You're up to something, aren't you?" she asks.

Troy picks up a pack of unfiltered Camels that is next to his keys and cell phone on the kitchen table. He takes a book of matches from the pocket of his gray flannel shirt. He shakes out a cigarette, sticks it in his mouth, and strikes a match. He draws the smoke in deep, releases it in a heavy sigh that makes a cloud between them.

"There's nothing going on," Troy says, leaning back and tapping an ash off his cigarette. "You know that," he adds.

"No, I *don't* know," says Rita. "You'll just have to tell me."

"I'm just thinking a lot these days," he says.

"Thinking? That's it—just *think*ing? About what, then, Mister Deep Thinker?" she demands.

Troy hesitates, then says, "Work, paying the bills, keeping my truck on the road another year. You know, about what's next."

"No, there's more to it than that," Rita says. "I'll tell you this: *what's next* is what we're going to talk about next."

Her eyes squint into his while he holds her gaze. Rita turns toward the window, looks out into the evening sky. "You're hiding something, and I *know* it," she says.

When Troy was working some overtime last week, Rita went through his two drawers in the dresser, rifling through his socks, his boxers, his sweaters, looking for a love note, a receipt for a gift, some proof of her suspicions. Coming up empty, she checked all the pockets in the pants hanging on hangers, followed by all the pockets in his jeans on the closet shelf. She even went through his coat pockets. Matchbooks, odd coins, a used Kleenex, a button. During the week, whenever he was showering, she copied out names and phone numbers from his cell on to an index card. She'd called them with a phone card from a pay phone at the pharmacy, hanging up when the person whose name matched the number answered. After the last call, she threw the index card and phone card in the trashcan next to the pay phone. *Damn*, she thought, *he's good*.

"That's so like you, Rita," Troy says. "You take everything personally."

"Well damn it, that's because I'm a *person*, something which *you* seem to forget, Mister I-keep-everything-to-myself. Typical *guy*." She taps her foot rapidly on the floor, and says, "Troy, I swear, sometimes you can be such a dick-head."

"Mountains out of mole hills," Troy replies, not looking up.

"Ex*cuse* me?" Rita replies.

"You make mountains out of mole hills, you always do."

"And just why would I want to do *that*?" she asks.

"Jealousy?" he says.

"What?" she stammers, "Me? Jealous? Jealous of *what*? " She picks a butter knife off the counter, fingers its dull tip, sets it in the sink. "And just what would I have to be jealous about, anyway?"

"That's for me to know and you to find out," he says.

"Just you quit trying to be funny," she says, getting louder.

"I'm not," he says.

"This is *serious*, Troy," she says.

"I'm being serious here," he says.

"Well I don't think so," Rita says, starting to pace up and down the narrow kitchen. "I think you're being ... evasive. Yeah, that's the word, *evasive*," she says, happy to have found the word. "I know you're *hiding* something from me," she adds. "Some secret you don't want me to know about."

Rita stops, faces him. She sets her Pepsi can on the counter and puts both hands on her hips, as if to corner him, block off any escape route Troy might consider taking. "And I intend to find out what it is. You *owe* me an answer," she announces.

His eyes shift from the newspaper to her eyes. He blinks slowly, glances at the paper. He turns back to her, taking a long drag on his cigarette until the ash falls from the tip onto the table, breaking, scattering. He rubs the cigarette out in the ashtray.

"I don't owe you squat," he smirks, crushing out the cigarette in the ashtray.

The small lamp on the kitchen table, plugged into a timer, lights instantly with a just-audible *pop*, startling them both. Each of their bodies involuntarily jerks, as if the house had shifted slightly, or as if the balls of their feet registered a minor tremor preceding a quake, or felt its aftershocks.

Troy reaches for his cigarettes and holds the pack in his hands. The matches remain on the table.

Rita is shaking slightly. She puts her hands flat on the table in front of Troy and looks him directly in the eyes. "I'll find out," she says, her voice steady, tight, hard. "And when I do, *mister*, I'll be gone. And you—you'll be sorry."

"We'll see," he says, turning back to the sports page.

"Oh yeah? And we'll see who's *gone*, too!" she says.

Rita turns on her heel and strides from the kitchenette toward the door. The clicking of her heels on the linoleum is followed by the sound of the screen door opening as she steps out into the night.

Troy shakes out a cigarette and lights it. The spent match, tossed into the cold coffee, hisses. On the table in front of him are the newspaper, his keys, his cell phone. He reaches for the keys, picks them up, sets them back down.

He hears Rita's Chevy start, listens as she pulls out of the driveway of the one bedroom bungalow. The car's headlights shine momentarily through the small kitchenette window. The lenses of his glasses, catching the light's glint, are like small mirrors illuminated by candles.

FIXING A HOLE

The drought had gone on for nearly four months. Every farmer from here to Sioux Falls was praying for relief. Bunch of guys over in Pierre paid some old Sioux Indian to do a rain dance up in the Black Hills, but it didn't do no good. The governor called in the Army Corp of Engineers. Cloud-seeding, they said, was the way to go. So they seeded for days.

The rain started. People up and down the street and all over town cheered like that thunderstorm was a parade coming down the street. Then it started to pour. Before you know it, it was raining so you couldn't hardly see your hand in front of your own face. Must have been a couple of inches an hour coming down. And it was *loud,* like hail on a metal roof.

My wife Mae was nervous and had me go get her mother from two blocks over and move her to higher ground. I took her over to her cousin Ella's, off I-90 heading toward Black Hawk. By the time I got back home, about midnight, the water was so deep in the street the truck stalled, and my Dodge sits up high, you know? I had to wade through near thigh-high water to get to the house. I'd never seen the likes of that before.

Once the water filled the Pactola dam that made Canyon Lake up above town, the earthen dam couldn't hold it. When it broke, the only place for the water to go was down. So it spilled into Rapid Creek, sluicing all at once like that into the canyon, turning into a flash flood beyond anything any of us could have imagined.

When that water come down the canyon, it looked like a fifty-foot high wall of water, like a tidal wave, or monster made of water right out of some Hollywood movie. And it was picking up speed. Tipped over an eighty-year-old maple we had in the yard, just like that. That water struck my house so hard the sheer force of it knocked it right off the foundation when it hit.

Me and the wife run up into the attic faster than the water could follow us. Mae struggled because the power was out and it was dark, so I had to guide her. We could feel the house moving like a drunken boat, then we smacked into something which turned out to be a pair of trees, and we stopped. I could feel the house settling and sinking so I laid on my back on the attic floor where it met the roof and I started kicking. Took what seemed like an hour, but I kicked a hole through the roof, with just my feet, else we'd've drowned. So me and Mae crawled out and there we sat, on the roof, getting soaked in the rain and looking like drowned rats. My feet hurt something fierce.

What was scary was we could see propane tanks that'd shook free from them cheap mobile homes up the canyon moving in the water, like torpedoes, as they come by. We watched one tank hit a house down the block there, or rather, where the house used to be. Saw another one blow Ed Haskett and his wife Lola clear the hell out of the tree they was sitting in. I can still see that ball of fire and hear them screaming sometimes when I wake up in the middle of the night.

This here foundation is where my house used to be. Now it just looks like a pool with steps. House is about a block-and-a-half down that way, wedged between two trees, else it would've washed farther than that. Lost my three-car garage and both the trucks from my construction business. Had a road grader, too; water twisted the son-of-a-bitch so it looked like a yellow licorice whip.

You go down to the Rushmore Tavern, you can still see a line on the wall running about chest-high where the water come in and filled the place. I'll tell you what, everybody in Rapid City lost something or somebody in that flood. Over two hundred and fifty people dead, hundreds of houses destroyed, thousands of cars and trucks ruined. That's what the papers said. Then add in the injuries, the loose dogs the National Guard shot during Marshall Law, and you get the picture.

Don't even talk to me about insurance companies. More than a hundred million in claims, and all they give back is dimes on the dollar. Left us so wiped out we can't buy coffee, let alone pay a deductible. Of course, the rich folks were OK. They always are, living higher up on the hill than working folk like us when a flood hits.

Look at me: I'm sixty-seven years old. I was getting ready to retire before that shit storm hit. What in the name of hell am I supposed to do now? Start all over again, like I was twenty? Who'd have thought a tidal wave would've hit Rapid City, South Dakota?

Mae and me've been talking. Well, she's been talking and I been listening. But we agree. We don't trust living by mountains no more. Think we've had enough of that. Maybe we'll take her mother and go someplace else where it's flat and safe. Like the South. Florida, Texas, Mississippi. Or maybe New Orleans.

She's Leaving Home

Elaine first dreamed of leaving when she was in the second year of her marriage. Alan, her husband, was a social worker who helped evicted families find shelter, and when the economy tumbled after the housing bubble burst, he was at the office too many nights and weekends. Left home alone so much, with a lot of time on her hands, it seemed to Elaine as if the walls were inching in on her in the silent house. As her thumb repeatedly pressed the remote, the TV displayed an endless array of images that enticed her to the vast green space of her desires: suburban communities where neighbors are friends, cities with pulsing dance clubs, or tropical ranches where lovers rode Palominos on the beach together. One morning after Alan had gone in early again to work, Elaine gathered what little she would need, pushed it into an empty suitcase, and left.

Within a month she was living in another city with a divorced man who had two spoiled children and high credit card debt. Though he had a nine-to-five job, he usually went in around ten and was back home by four. He had a lot of time for Elaine and she warmed in the glow of his attention. Weekends, they sat on the deck drinking frozen daiquiris and listening to soft jazz on the radio. They ate out at chain restaurants almost every night and began planning a cruise. One afternoon Elaine came home from her job as a lunch hour restaurant hostess to find the foyer filled with the divorced man and his two children's suitcases, packed for the cruise. Hers, packed for her with what she had brought, was waiting by the door like an old dog. When her divorced man's jealous ex-wife had found out about the cruise, she'd met him secretly, convincing him to throw Elaine out so she could be re-installed both in her four bedroom castle and on the deck chair. Elaine knew if she had paid attention, she might have seen it coming. So she went, her heels pocking like a dog's toenails across the stone floor to the door.

The dream of returning came to her while she was opening the trunk of her Neon to load her suitcase and a bag of organic apples. When she turned the key, a country and western station started playing. Alan—she would go home to Alan: she was displaced, evicted in a sense, who else was better to turn to? He had always loved her, so she believed he must love her still. She would return to her place at the kitchen table, to her side of the bed, to her previous life. She wistfully imagined him sitting at the kitchen table, an uneaten peanut butter and jelly sandwich turning stale as he sighed for the eleven hundredth time while looking out the window at the garage wall.

The drive home seemed longer than she remembered it taking when she left, and even when she arrived in town, she was uncertain about which was the best route to the house. When she found the street, she drove past the house and had to park a few driveways down the street and walk back. She could hear the sprinkler across the street as she walked up the sidewalk. The house looked different than she remembered, more like the rest of the houses, less like hers and Alan's, though the house number was right and her key fit the lock.

When she entered, the house lights were on, but no one was home. It was silent except for the ticking of the kitchen clock. At the table, she found two bowls emptied of soup, and a box of saltines with only one packet remaining. One of the two wine glasses had a hoop earring hooked around the stem. A small plate holding the core from a pared apple told the rest. Elaine imagined lipstick on one of the apple slices.

After leaving the subdivision behind, she came to a four way stop. A few drops of rain tapped on the windshield and the wind whistled slightly through the just-opened passenger door window. As she waited at the red light, the Neon idling, the dream of the sequel arrived. If she turned right, it would take her to her sister's where she could stay until she figured out what to do next. Going straight, she would get to the state route that took her to the divorced man's house where she could ask to be taken back. If she turned around, she could return to Alan and ask to be taken back. If she turned left, it would take her to the interstate highway where the choice was a future just as uncertain if she went east or west. Elaine gripped the steering wheel. She looked at the red light, saw how the side lights of the traffic signal were turning from green to yellow. Then her light changed to green.

Here Comes the Sun

Jay took up birding late in life. When he turned fifty-three, his girlfriend Robin gave him a *Peterson Guide* and a nesting box. "You've got to get out of the house more," she told him, "or that cholesterol's gonna kill you, regardless of how much red wine you drink." Even though Jay thought the whole idea was for bird-brains, he figured he'd give it a try to keep Robin happy.

That first summer, they had a brood of six tree swallows. By the second summer he'd added five boxes to his trail in the park, and he fledged eleven bluebirds and nine tree swallows. By the fourth year, Jay was going to Pelee Island for the Hawkwatch, to Nebraska for Sandhill Cranes, and to the Everglades where cormorants, anhingas, and ospreys were wintering.

One August, he is standing with Robin in a cattail marsh on Presque Isle, watching purple Martins gather. He's pricing out in his head what two weeks in Belize would cost when he notices his shoulder blades are bothering him. Robin's *Oh-oh* as she feels his back makes him remove his Eddie Bauer all-cotton wilderness shirt so she can have a better look. "Looks like you're sprouting, Jay," she observes, concerned.

His doctor confirms what he suspected: he's actually growing small wings—white ones, maybe seven inches long—from his shoulder blades.

"They may stay and grow," his doctor says. "It's like those freak kids born now and then with tails."

While the doctor recommends surgery, and Robin suggests larger shirts (she finds it a little sexy, after all), Jay is uncertain.

Jay stands on his back porch the next morning at sunrise, not having slept much during the night. The coffee cup warms his hands.

Facing north, he thinks he can scent the coming winter. The migration is beginning. He needs to be ready. The little wings are lifting and falling, lifting and falling, turning him toward the south.

A Day in the Life

Vito Presti, Mister Little Italy, had the best prices for eight days and seven nights, accommodations and air fare included.

That spring we thought we could add some spice to our relationship. A little cooking, a little stirring.

The place we stayed was a second floor walkup run by a Sicilian grandmother named Anna who dreamed of dark chocolate, former lovers, biscotti, and grandchildren.

The restaurant felt more like a large kitchen in a home.

The tour takes you up in the mountains to the edge of the local volcano, which is still active.

All over Perugia are houses with fake painted windows.

In Verona, they brought us a dish with calamari called *Romeo's Lips* which is served with a dry red wine called *Juliet's Nurse*.

You sat on the stone wall. Your legs, showing sandal straps, looked like two straws drinking from the fountain below the marble archangel by the old cathedral. You hadn't said a word since dinner, and frankly, I wasn't expecting you to.

As the moon rose over the bay above the small fishing boats, I smoked those French cigarettes that smelled like cloves and drank the cheap local Chianti from the lips of a basketed bottle. I was struck dumb, my mouth open wider than a boat, as I realized you held more secrets than the vaults in the Vatican.

"After the olive oil is heated," the chef said, "add two cloves of garlic, a handful of fresh basil, uncut, and three seeded tomatoes, then cook for two minutes before adding the shrimp just long enough for them to pink. And," he added, wagging his finger at us like a celery stalk, "serve it over angel-hair pasta, or don't serve it at all."

In Venice, our gondoliers wore polyester striped shirts with soiled white slacks and sang cheesy Italian versions of American pop songs. You wore your orange faux tam, but you looked a bit green around the gills, I thought, from the way the boat lurched, while I had indigestion from all that garlic on the roasted artichokes we'd had for lunch.

The responsibility for the recipe rests squarely on the shoulders of the pastry chef.

Coming from the same biological family, the rose has become a symbol for all flowers, as the apple has become the symbol for all fruits.

Many of the ancient stone structures have collapsed. Some from violence, some from stress.

During Lent, almonds and vanilla make the best cakes. You can get a good price in the market for them. In the piazza, we watched the old men dunk the cakes in a sweet wine.

Since a weather front was moving through, and the morning's showers were still lurking about, we had to cancel the car.

Your hair fell across your face. The moonlight coming in from the open door to the balcony fell across your face. Your shadow fell across me on the bed. I was wondering how to say *done* in Italian.

MAGICAL MYSTERY TOUR

Harry fell under a magic spell at his cousin Louis' eleventh birthday party. Weegie the clown who was hired for entertainment wasn't very funny, but he could do magic tricks. He pulled a rabbit out of a hat. Doves flew from his sleeves. Watches went under a black cloth into a world of nothingness, and while everyone waited, they never reappeared. Harry had entered a world of poetry and wonder. Harry was hooked.

While the clown was packing up to go, Harry tapped him on the elbow.

"You're the best magician in the world," he said.

Weegie laughed. "No kid," he said, "I just do tricks." And with that, he took off his red rubber nose, held it up in his left hand, covered it with his right hand, then opened his empty left hand.

"Where'd it go?" Harry asked.

The clown put his right hand against Harry's head and pulled a bright green silk handkerchief from Harry's left ear. "Sleight of hand, kid," Weegie said. "That's all magic is: illusions and presti-digitations."

Harry sent for a catalog from Murphy's Magic Shop and soon had a collapsible top hat, linking rings, and a deck of special cards. He practiced in front of the mirror until his reflection had the tricks down pat.

By the time he was fifteen, he was performing at birthday parties. He dressed like a real magician in his black cape. When he tipped his top hat at the end of shows, everyone gave him a hand.

Mothers walked arm-in-arm with him, introducing him to the guests and grandparents. Winking fathers paid him in cash. Older sisters paid him attention. It was as if he had pulled celebrity out of a hat.

The summer after he graduated from high school, he decided to go pro. He landed a job on a cruise ship. For the next two years, he entertained bored children and sunburned couples from St. Kits to Cancun, pulling bunnies from hats and making metal rings come apart and go back together. Flowers emerged from closed hands, eggs were pulled from his mouth, fires danced in the palms of his hands. He could even make bottles of champagne disappear to the gasps of the tourists, and he could make them reappear back in his room to the amazement of a blur of sultry divorcees who stuffed their bras with Southern accents.

Harry felt he was ready for prime time. He met with an agent, dreaming of doing late-night TV with Fallon, O'Brien, and Letterman, then long runs in Las Vegas.

"You're good, kid," agent Jimmy Slick told him, "but you're a two-pitch punk from the minor leagues who'll never break into the majors."

"But what about the disappearing champagne trick?" asked Harry.

"Kreskin can make a fuggin plane go away," Slick said, "and Blaine was frozen in ice for 63 hours. Even if you pulled those eggs from your ass, you'll still never make Vegas. Stick to birthday parties and getting laid by spinster aunts." The agent shook his head and walked away.

For the next month Harry practiced making bottles of bourbon disappear. One night he decided that if he couldn't achieve fame for doing the tricks himself, he would become famous for exposing how the other magicians did them. He'd show the bastards.

Within a week of hiring a new agent, Mr. Slycker, his pilot episode was accepted by FOX and he had his own show, *Truth or Illusion.* The first week it aired, Harry showed how Houdini escaped from chains while submerged in a tank of water. He taught a seven-year-old child how to pull a coin from his little sister's ear, and the show ended with the entire audience performing the same trick on the count of three. Harry had pulled a hit from his hat.

Over the next few weeks, he showed how doves were hidden in sleeves and rabbits in hats, how women were sawn in half, and how he could levitate or disappear in plain view inside the spinning cabinet. Mr. Slycker signed him to a multimillion dollar contract, and details appeared as if from nowhere: action figures, video games, his own line of magic kits, even an option on a biopic. There was no escaping fame now.

Harry was in his dressing room at the Ed Sullivan Theater in New York getting ready for a show that would expose how David Copperfield, the richest magician in history, made the Statue of Liberty disappear. He was considering whether the next episode would show how Copperfield levitated over the Grand Canyon or how David Blaine managed to stand for thirty-five hours on top of a pillar in Bryant Park in New York City. "I'll bring 'em all down," he said, as he passed a small flame back and forth between his hands.

A man wearing a black cape suddenly appeared in the chair next to him. Harry jumped up, surprised.

"How did you get in?" he asked

"It's a magic trick," the man said. "You tell me."

"What do you want?" Harry asked.

"Listen, kid. You have to stop exposing other magicians' tricks," he said, his hands together as if he was holding something in them. "It's against the professional code. I speak for everyone at Magicians and Illusionists Local 123. Stop what you're doing. People's livelihoods are on the line."

"Get out," Harry said, "and go back to doing birthday parties. You have illusions, but I have the power of truth."

"Beware the power of consequences," the man said, and disappeared.

"I could do that trick when I was ten," Harry told the empty room as he left for the studio.

That night Harry got his highest Neilson ratings. More people watched his show than watched the NCAA Basketball finals.

Rupert Murdock made a special appearance and pulled a piglet from a hat, just as Harry had taught him to do.

That evening Harry owned the world. He was the star of the show, the moon of illusion, and the sun of truth.

Leaving to the applause of the studio crew and fans, he bowed and tipped his top hat, releasing a dozen white doves. Then he turned, stepped out the door of the theater into the dark alley where he vanished into thin air.

ACKNOWLEDGMENTS CONTINUED

The author would like to thank the following publications in which many of these works of fiction first appeared, sometimes in different form and mostly with other titles.

"Norwegian Wood" (as "The Gardner's Tale") in *Bellingham Review*; "Blackbird" (as "Hope is the Feathered Thing") in *Apple Valley Review*; "Ticket to Ride" (as "Three's a Crowd") in *Istanbul Literary Review*; "Matchbox" (as "Pyromania: A Love Story") in *Stray Dog*; "Here Comes the Sun" (as "True South") in *Hamilton Stone Review*; "Penny Lane" (as "Camelot") in *Mochila Review*; "Baby's in Black" (as "The Red Bandana") in *Ophelia Street*; "Maxwell's Silver Hammer" (as "Elvis Presley's Greatest Hits") in *The Arden*; "While My Guitar Gently Weeps" as "Paperboy" in *The Seamless Serial Hour* (Pudding House Press); "Good Day Sunshine" (as "Emperor of Light") in *Muse* [The Lit]; "A Day in the Life" (as "La Pensione: A Romance") in *Rock the Boat* (All Nations Press); "The White Album"(as "White Noise") in *Cup of Fiction*; "Paperback Writer" (as "Report Card") in *Queen Mab & the Moon Boy* (Kattywompus Press); "Hello Goodbye" (as "Electric Boulevard") in *Mystic River Review*; "Magical Mystery Tour" and "Nowhere Man" in *Buried Letter Press*; "We Can Work It Out" (as "John Chapman") in *Box of Light* (Pudding House Press); "Rain" in *Storyglossia*; "Get Back" (as "Lost and Found Treasures of Noble's Pond") in *Growing Up: Persons, Places, and Things* (Cleveland State University/Poets & Writers League of Greater Cleveland) ; "Strawberry Fields Forever," published as "Blue Christmas" in *Christmas Stories from Ohio* (Kent State University Press).

ABOUT THE AUTHOR

Robert Miltner Miltner was born in Cleveland and raised in Avon Lake, along Lake Erie on the north coast of Ohio. He's lived most of his life in Ohio, at various times in Cincinnati, Steubenville, Lakewood, Little Italy, and Canton. He has attended Xavier University for a B.A., John Carroll University for a M.Ed., and Kent State University for a Ph.D.

He is Associate Professor of English at Kent State University at Stark where he teaches creative writing and literature. He is on the poetry faculty of, and is the Kent State University Campus Coordinator for the Northeast Ohio MFA in Creative Writing Consortium Program (NEOMFA). He has been an active advocate for peace and justice.

His collection of prose poems, *Hotel Utopia*, was selected by National Book Award Finalist Tim Seibles as winner of the New Rivers Press book prize and was a finalist for the Ohioana Book Award in Poetry; he is also the author of fifteen chapbooks and limited editions, including *Against the Simple* (Wick chapbook award) and *Eurydice Rising* (Red Berry Editions award). Miltner's poems, fiction, and essays have appeared widely in a variety of literary magazines including in *Wisconsin Review, Prose Poem, Birmingham Poetry Review, New York Quarterly, Artful Dodge, Bellingham Review, Journal of the Short Story in English, AWP Chronicle, Dictionary of Literary Biography*, and others. He is co-founder of the International Raymond Carver Society and edits *The Raymond Carver Review*.

RECENT BOOKS BY BOTTOM DOG PRESS

BOOKS IN THE HARMONY SERIES
And Your Bird Can Sing
By Robert Miltner, 122 pgs. $16
Echo: Poems
By Christina Lovin, 114 pgs. $16
Stolen Child: A Novel
By Suzanne Kelly, 338 pgs. $18
The Canary : A Novel
By Michael Loyd Gray, 196 pgs. $18
On the Flyleaf: Poems
By Herbert Woodward Martin, 106 pgs. $16
The Harmonist at Nightfall: Poems of Indiana
By Shari Wagner, 114 pgs. $16
Painting Bridges: A Novel
By Patricia Averbach, 234 pgs. $18
Ariadne & Other Poems
By Ingrid Swanberg, 120 pgs. $16
The Search for the Reason Why: New and Selected Poems
By Tom Kryss, 192 pgs. $16
Kenneth Patchen: Rebel Poet in America
By Larry Smith, Revised 2nd Edition, 326 pgs. Cloth $28
Selected Correspondence of Kenneth Patchen,
Edited with introduction by Allen Frost, Paper $18/ Cloth $28
Awash with Roses: Collected Love Poems of Kenneth Patchen
Eds. Laura Smith and Larry Smith, 200 pgs. $16

HARMONY COLLECTIONS AND ANTHOLOGIES
d.a.levy and the mimeograph revolution
Eds. Ingrid Swanberg and Larry Smith, 276 pgs. $20
Come Together: Imagine Peace
Eds. Ann Smith, Larry Smith, Philip Metres, 204 pgs. $16
Evensong: Contemporary American Poets on Spirituality
Eds. Gerry LaFemina and Chad Prevost, 240 pgs. $16
America Zen: A Gathering of Poets
Eds. Ray McNiece and Larry Smith, 224 pgs. $16
Family Matters: Poems of Our Families
Eds. Ann Smith and Larry Smith, 232 pgs. $16

Bottom Dog Press, Inc.
PO Box 425/ Huron, Ohio 44839
Order Online at:
http://smithdocs.net/BirdDogy/BirdDogPage.html

Recent Books by Bottom Dog Press

Books in the Working Lives Series
An Act of Courage: Poems By Mort Krahling,
Eds. Judy Platz and Brooke Horvath, 104 pgs. $16
Story Hour & Other Stories
By Robert Flanagan, 122 pgs. $16
Sky Under the Roof: Poems
By Hilda Downer, 126 pgs. $16
Breathing the West: Great Basin Poems
By Liane Ellison Norman, 80 pgs. $16
Smoke: Poems By Jeanne Bryner, 96 pgs. $16
Maggot : A Novel By Robert Flanagan, 262 pgs. $18
Broken Collar: A Novel By Ron Mitchell, 234 pgs. $18
American Poet: A Novel By Jeff Vande Zande, 200 pgs. $18
The Pattern Maker's Daughter: Poems
By Sandee Gertz Umbach, 90 pages $16
The Way-Back Room: Memoir of a Detroit Childhood
By Mary Minock, 216 pgs. $18
The Free Farm: A Novel By Larry Smith, 306 pgs. $18
Sinners of Sanction County: Stories
By Charles Dodd White, 160 pgs. $17
Learning How: Stories, Yarns & Tales
By Richard Hague, 216 pgs. $18
Strangers in America: A Novel
By Erika Meyers, 140 pgs. $16
Riders on the Storm: A Novel
By Susan Streeter Carpenter, 404 pgs. $18
The Long River Home: A Novel
By Larry Smith, 230 pgs. Paper $16/ Cloth $22
Landscape with Fragmented Figures: A Novel
By Jeff Vande Zande, 232 pgs. $16
The Big Book of Daniel: Collected Poems
By Daniel Thompson, 340 pgs. Paper $18/ Cloth $22;
Reply to an Eviction Notice: Poems
By Robert Flanagan, 100 pgs. $15
An Unmistakable Shade of Red & The Obama Chronicles
By Mary E. Weems, 80 pgs. $15
Our Way of Life: Poems By Ray McNiece, 128 pgs. $15

Bottom Dog Press, Inc.
PO Box 425/ Huron, Ohio 44839
Order Online at:
http://smithdocs.net/BirdDogy/BirdDogPage.html